A DIAMOND QUINTET

by

ANTHONY DALTON

A DIAMOND QUINTET

© Anthony Dalton, 2018
All rights reserved.

ISBN 13: 9781980691624

Cover design by Steve Crowhurst

Background cover images courtesy of storyblocks.com

Photograph of arm and hand on front cover © Anthony Dalton
Photograph of Namib Desert scene on back cover © Anthony Dalton

Font: Garamond 12

Published by Anthony Dalton Books

Thank you for buying an authorized copy of this book and for complying with copyright laws by not reproducing, scanning, or distributing any part of it in any form without written permission from the author. In doing so you are supporting all writers.

For
all the Belgians who made our years in
Antwerp such a wonderful experience.

A DIAMOND QUINTET

CONTENTS

Cast of Characters

BOOK 1
A Magnificent Blue Diamond

BOOK 2
Hollywood

BOOK 3
A Gathering of Thieves

BOOK 4
The Rendezvous

BOOK 5
The Reprise

EPILOGUE
The Denouement

Cast of main Characters

Franz Kessler, a cattleman in South West Africa

Manny Goldstein, Diamond dealer in Windhoek, South West Africa.

Piet de Kerpel, master diamond cutter in Antwerp, Belgium

Richard Campbell, Hollywood film director

Sandy Anders, Actress, producer

Robert Cochrane, Hollywood film producer

Antonio Carlos Riviero y Perez. Known as **Tango Perez**. Costa Rican polo player and playboy.

Ali Ben Rachid, Algerian living in USA. A university student, pickpocket; jewel thief

April Young, American jewel thief

Yusuf Tyfor, Algerian small-arms dealer and terrorist living in Paris, France.

Rupert Allen, English antiques dealer

Charles Berglund, American antiques dealer living in England

Chris Montague, English actor

Senor Fuentes, Bank manager in San Jose, Costa Rica

Carlos Gutierrez, Manservant to Tango Perez

Nick Gradowski, American freelance photographer

Samantha Walker, English journalist

Ingrid Strauss, Diamond Centre administrator, Antwerp, Belgium

Inspector Etienne Delvaux, Belgian police officer based in Antwerp, Belgium

Wim Cijfers, curator at the Diamond Museum, Antwerp, Belgium

Jack Philmore, FBI Agent, Washington, D.C.

BOOK 1

A Magnificent Blue Diamond

Chapter 1   **The Namib Desert, 1936**

The searing mid-day temperatures of the northern Namib Desert sent waves of moisture-sucking heat shimmering over the land. The haze generated by a blistering sun and scorching sand stretched to and obliterated the horizon. The sky turned from deep blue overhead to stark white as it reached to touch the land, which gradually turned from the same stark white to yellow gold. Along the base of a giant sand dune a thin grey demarcation line was broken only by a single thorny acacia tree, and the slow-moving form of a stately old oryx.

To the west the great red, pink, and orange dunes of the Namib Desert formed a virtually impenetrable barrier between the ocean and the land. South, the desert stretched to the South African border and beyond. North, the dunes repeated their patterns of stars and crescents all the way to the Cunene River. In the east, the wilderness of sand, stones, and hardy shrubs, merged into the equally formidable Kalahari Desert. It was a land where death lay in wait for the unwary.

An oryx, or gemsbok, to some the most elegant gazelle in Africa, endowed by nature with the ability to withstand enormously high temperatures without losing significant amounts of water, plodded slowly through the wilderness. Behind, in an almost straight line reaching back to the horizon, its tracks – like large parallel teardrops – marked its passage. The oryx roamed on, undeterred by the heat. Its life was reaching its conclusion. It was alone. Soon it would find somewhere to settle down and drift into the merciful peace of oblivion.

In the distant haze half a dozen ostriches strutted in self-important silence over the land. A sidewinder adder, no more than a man's foot in length when stretched, lay almost buried under the sand near a dead bush. Occasionally it flicked out its forked tongue to taste the scents borne on the air. Patiently it watched and waited in the sparse shade for an unwary long-tailed lizard to pass by.

As the oryx steadily picked its way over jagged pebbles shattered by the unrelenting heat of eternity, one scarred hoof kicked aside a smooth, dull rock the size of a small fist. The uneven stone turned and rolled unsteadily a short way, presenting a side unexposed to wind and weather for generations. It sparkled, as if in imitation of the sun and the stars. It reflected the colour of the sky. The oryx, a weary veteran with no need of such baubles, saw little except the sand and rapidly approaching death. It took no notice as it left the stone upturned.

A slight, barely visible irregularity on the crest of a dune changed shape as a black-backed jackal trotted into view. Its acute sense of smell had picked up the old oryx from the valley on the other side. Knowing by instinct that death was not far away, it tracked the large beast patiently. When the oryx finally succumbed to the inevitable, the hungry jackal would not be far away. With a little luck it would be able to snatch a meal before the vultures descended in a greedy flock and the inevitable scavenging hyenas arrived to pick the carcass clean.

The seasons rotated through four annual cycles. No rain fell. The only moisture to reach the desert came in on the occasional sea fogs, blown in by cool South Atlantic winds. Before the sun could heat and evaporate the minute droplets of water, all the plants and insects; every creature of the sand absorbed the life sustaining liquid. A tenebrionid beetle, the one Afrikaners call kopstaan, welcomed each fog as a life saver. It condensed the miniscule airborne water supply on its sloping back, before up-ending itself to allow the moisture to flow along tiny grooves to its mouth so life could go on.

A giant welwitschia, after close to two thousand years of life, one of the oldest living plants on earth, lay baking on the desert's surface. The long tough leaves split, frayed, and disintegrated at the ends, while at their base they constantly renewed as their cells divided. Far under the sand an enormous taproot drew the plant's needs from the moisture trapped beneath the desert. The fog gave it little, other than a brief respite from the clinging dust. Close to the main plant a single fertile seed began to wake from its dormant state as the droplets gave it the beginning of a long and sedentary life.

In the lee of a giant boomerang-shaped barchan dune an Ovambo herdsman knelt by bleached bones. Holding the oryx skull down with his foot, he twisted one long, graceful horn sharply, removing it from the sun-bleached white bone. Approvingly he sighted along the ribbed length of the near straight horn. Grunting in acceptance, he tucked the prize into his leather waist strap and removed the second horn. It too was in top condition. He placed it with the first. If he was lucky he would be able to sell both to a white man for a few shiny coins.

Trailing behind the herdsman his two scrawny cows gave the carcass a wide berth. They were too close to death themselves to want to be reminded so vividly of its finality. There was no grass, no tasty green shoots; no soothing water.

Moaning unhappily, the cattle followed their master round the dune. The herdsman walked leisurely to conserve his own energy and the remaining strength of his cattle. As he placed one bare, dust-covered foot in front of the other, he kept his eyes downcast, watching for tell-tale signs. Somewhere beneath the sand, perhaps deep down, there had to be water. Occasionally he stopped and scratched at the dry surface. With his hands he swept aside the loose sand, testing the hard-packed soil beneath for any sign of moisture. Somewhere nearby, he knew, although he had never been this far west before, there had to be a series

3

of small underground springs: other desert travellers had told him so.

In a slight depression he found three wild watermelon plants. There was no fruit left on them, not even the slightly oily seeds which would have nourished him a little. They were dead, victims of the long drought. Disappointed and hungry the old Ovambo lay down on the sand to rest until the worst of the heat faded. He pulled his torn loin cloth over his head and went to sleep.

The sun was low when he awoke. Nearby his cows waited with drooping heads. Slowly the herdsman got to his feet, twisting his ankle slightly on a stone. He reached down and picked it up, holding it at arm's length against the sky. The setting sun played its softening colours over the surface, casting them deep into the stone itself. Miniature beams of blue light, streaked with the sun's dying orange, flashed as he turned the stone this way and that, examining it from all angles. Fascinated with his find, he tucked it into his cloth near the belt, arranging it so he was comfortable. Then, followed by his cows, he continued his lonely journey.

Late in the afternoon, the day after his discovery, a slight breeze rustled the Ovambo's dusty, grey hair. He turned and sniffed the air. Beside him his cattle too were searching the gentle wind for any hint of the moisture they needed so badly. The Ovambo inhaled deeply, turning his head to follow the faint scent as he did so. He smiled, his wrinkled face creasing even more with pleasure. Borne on the late afternoon's final breaths there was the unmistakable tang of fresh water. It was not far away; just beyond the closest dune.

Franz Kessler shaded his eyes with the brim of his hat. Behind him the large herd of cattle jostled each other inside the makeshift compound as they waited for their turn at the water trough. He had found the springs some years before and used them to water the herd he was taking south. Each year since then he had stopped at the same water source. Up ahead, beside a dune, Kessler thought he saw a movement. He stood up in his stirrups for a better look. Last night, when he rested by his small fire, the distinctive deep-throated groans of a hunting pride of lions had broken the silence. He'd lost four cows in the past weeks to predators and he couldn't afford to lose more. Most of the herd belonged to his employer. Kessler would have to pay for any losses on the trail out of his own few cows. With night rapidly approaching again he needed to be extra vigilant.

In the distance the movement became a man followed by two cows. Kessler watched as the skinny black man slowly, steadily, approached. The limping native greeted him with a raised hand then pointed to the water trough and back to his thirsty charges. Kessler nodded.

The Ovambo gratefully watered his animals. Cupping his hands together to form a bowl, he drank a few sips himself. Kessler continued to ride round his own herd scanning the darkening eastern horizon as he went. The Ovambo herdsman wiped both hands on his cloth. Reaching into his belt he drew the two oryx horns and held them high.

"Baas," he called.

Kessler turned in the saddle, saw what the herdsman held and shook his head. Unperturbed the old man tucked the horns back into his belt.

"Baas!" he called again. This time he held the stone in one hand, high above his head where the fading light could catch it. Kessler turned his mount and went to look. He reached out and the old man passed the stone to him. Kessler turned it over in his hand. Trying not to show his rising excitement he held the stone up to the setting sun.

"Mein Gott," he muttered, "Where did you find this?"

The Ovambo pointed aimlessly into the distance. He held his other hand out for his stone.

"What do you want for it?" Kessler asked, tossing it lightly in his hand, feeling the weight. The Ovambo looked longingly at Kessler's cattle, then back to the stone.

"You want one of my cows. Is that it?"

A glottal click was his reply.

"I could shoot you and take your miserable cows and your stone. No one would know."

The dark brown hand, with dusky palm uppermost, thrust up at Kessler. "Give me back my stone," it ordered. Obsidian eyes bored into his without fear. For a long moment the two men glared at each other, neither willing to make the first move: neither willing to back off.

Kessler considered his options. Shooting the old Ovambo had been an idle threat, nothing more. His strong Lutheran upbringing kept him from harming the man. He could, of course, just take the stone and ride away with it. One old native on foot couldn't do him much harm, brave though he obviously was.

The diamond, he was positive that's what he held, should be worth a fortune. He knew a cow was little enough to pay for such a treasure.

"Okay, old man. It's only a joke. I'll give you a cow."

The Ovambo held up two fingers and pointed at the herd. He stared up at Kessler, determined to earn a just payment.

"You want two of my cows? What makes you think your stone's worth two of my cattle?"

Once again, the Ovambo held up two fingers. His eyes narrowed to creases and he took a step closer towards Kessler's horse. He pointed back at the herd, picking out two cows before holding the same two fingers up to Kessler again.

"Two cows, for this stone? Well, you've got balls. I'll say that for you, old man."

Kessler stowed the stone in his saddlebag. With a grin at the waiting native he turned and rode into his herd. Effortlessly he cut out the two cows the old man had selected. They weren't the best of the herd by any means, but they were in far better condition than the Ovambo's two half-starved beasts.

"Here you go. Two fine healthy animals. Now be off with you."

With that he went back to studying the rapidly darkening horizon as if the encounter had never taken place. The native and his four cows ambled away to the north-west, in the direction of Sesfontein, the sun's final rays briefly lighting their flanks. They went without a backward glance.

Kessler thought about setting off for Windhoek immediately. Night and his own natural caution restrained him. He tethered his horse before checking his temporary fence of acacia branches, finding no obvious weak spots. It would do for one night, he decided. Expertly he built a simple fire a short distance away from the kraal and brewed a pot of thick black coffee. From one of his saddlebags he took out a hunk of stale bread and dunked it in his steaming mug. He sucked on the warm, damp bread, unperturbed by the dull taste. His mind was focused on the diamond.

Somewhere in the night a hyena chuckled, breaking into Kessler's thoughts. He listened for a while as another picked up the high-pitched giggling and answered. The cattleman threw another piece of wood on his fire and let his mind drift back to the diamond. Already he was planning the great kraal he would build to contain the huge herd of cattle he would soon own. In the kraal, on a rise shaded by a few tall, elegant, spreading jacaranda trees, his sprawling ranch house – with veranda on all sides – would stand like a palace. For a long time after he finished his meagre supper, he sat dreaming by the fire with the diamond in his hands. The warm red and orange flames flickered coldly through the gem as he examined his treasure from all angles.

A grumble, which started high, sounding like 'uuuh-huuumph' and tailing off to a much lower tone and deep groans, followed by the anxious lowing of his cattle and a nervous whinny from his horse, brought him back to the present. Stuffing the diamond into his saddlebag, Kessler grabbed his Mannlicher rifle with one hand and a burning brand from the fire with the other.

"Where are you, you bloody scavengers?" he shouted, holding the living torch high and looking around the circle of light. Behind him his horse snorted, dancing with fear, straining at its tether. The cattle milled about the enclosure in indecision, too frightened to run; too frightened to stay still.

"Whoa, Kaiser," Kessler called softly. "Whoa, boy. I'm here."

The lions were invisible, hidden in the darkness beyond the reach of the yellow flame. From the distinctive groans, Kessler guessed there were at least three females, maybe more. Somewhere out there, waiting for his mates to catch his dinner for him, was the larger, dark-maned male.

Kessler tossed the brand back into the fire and closed his eyes for a second to adjust to the dark. Quickly he scooped up his bag and slung it over his saddle. For long seconds he stood beside his horse, soothing him with soft words.

"Steady, Kaiser. Steady."

The predatory lions growled again, making the cattle even more agitated. Kaiser stamped his feet impatiently, wanting only to flee. Kessler held his reins in one hand and untied him with the other, still holding his rifle.

"Easy now," he breathed as he vaulted into the saddle and turned his mount away from the acacia kraal. "Easy now," he repeated as he reined Kaiser in, waiting. The night was pitch-black. Another two hours were needed before the welcoming light of a half-moon would brighten the sky. Two more hours of full dark.

Kessler leaned forward and stroked Kaiser's neck. "Good boy," he whispered. "Stay still. Keep calm. It's okay."

Kaiser trembled under him, waves of tension rippling across his skin. Kessler gripped tightly with his knees, dropped the reins in his lap and raised his rifle. He tucked it into his shoulder, comforted by the smooth wooden stock against his cheek. A tawny shape raced towards him from out of the blackness, its eyes glowing like the embers of his fire. Kessler sighted down the barrel and fired as Kaiser reared in alarm. The lioness screamed and somersaulted twice before crumpling to the dust a few metres away. Kaiser spun in a circle, prancing on hind legs, forelegs flailing at the sharp-clawed enemy close to his feet. Dimly Kessler saw another speeding shape clear the fence to his left with ease. He swung in an arc, squeezing the trigger as he turned. The bullet fanned the cat's fur without doing damage.

The cattle, already terrified at the proximity of the lions and their menacing voices, stampeded as the big cat landed on the back of one of their number. Within seconds the acacia fence was trampled and the herd, many streaming rivulets of dark blood from the millions of sharp thorns, raced into the night. Kessler aimed at the dim shape of the lioness astride the doomed cow's spine and shot her in the back of the head. The high-powered impact of the 9.5mm bullet knocked both creatures to the ground in a confused tangle of legs and bodies. A third lioness rushed to help her companion. Wicked jaws fastened on the cow's throat as it fell. Kessler fired again, catching the cat in the middle of its chest. She screamed once, high, pain filled, final. Without a pause, Kessler turned Kaiser's head and galloped after his charges. Fortunately, they had kept together in their fright, running until their lungs could take no more.

They stood in a group a kilometre away, steam rising in a sudden warm fog from sweaty backs, heads down and tongues hanging from open mouths like wet, pink slippers. As their panic subsided a few of the younger animals wandered off in search of grazing. By the time Kessler caught up with the main herd there were six missing. It took him much of the rest of the night to round them up and lead the herd back to his water trough.

The fallen cow was gone, dragged away to be consumed by the survivors of the pride. The three dead lionesses had suffered a similar fate, no doubt Kessler thought, from the hyenas he heard laughing callously in the distance.

Exhausted though he was after a day and a night without rest, Kessler painstakingly rebuilt the kraal. With his cattle safe once again he settled to the ground and fell instantly asleep. For three hours he lay there on the sand without moving, until the heat from the rising sun forced him awake.

"Now, we go south to Windhoek," he told his cattle as he got stiffly to his feet.

Between Kessler and the distant town stretched a vast wasteland of dunes, aeolian sand, gravel plains, and occasional stands of hardy shrubs and scattered acacias. A chain of waterholes, enough for his cattle's needs, dotted his route. Other creatures, both herbivores and carnivores, drank from the same pools. At no time on his long journey would he have a chance to relax.

Kessler showed no concern as he led his herd from the temporary kraal. The lions which had attacked in the night, those that had survived, had eaten well and were unlikely to follow. Though there were more dangers ahead, he whistled loudly to himself, a big smile on his weather-beaten young face as he went back to daydreaming about the money he would earn from the sale of the diamond.

For some days he followed the south bank of the dry bed of the Hoanib River. Each night he stopped to build a temporary kraal to contain his herd. He sat there, in front of a glowing fire, caressing his diamond until he fell asleep from exhaustion. Eventually he turned his cattle due south through a rocky landscape. On each side of the trail sunburnt hills glowed red under the fierce heat of daylight. A troop of chacma baboons watched from a ridge as the slow-moving herd kicked up clouds of dust in a broad canyon. Kessler tilted the brim of his hat up and counted the apes.

"Twenty-two," he said to himself, well aware that where there were baboons there were often lions. On an impulse he stood in his stirrups, cupped his hands around his mouth like a megaphone and gave a succession of harsh barks. The troop chattered and screamed excitedly, crowding around their leader. He, an old male with an almost black coat and grey beard, stood on his hind legs and barked in return, answering the implied challenge. Kessler barked again, louder. The troop scattered, their bright pink rumps disappearing beyond the ridge. The leader watched Kessler curiously. Twice more they barked at each other. Kessler's horse stamped its hooves impatiently.

"Okay, Kaiser. It's okay," Kessler spoke soothingly without taking his eyes off the old baboon. Ahead the cattle and their attendant dust cloud kept moving, oblivious to all but the trail. Deciding the man was no threat, the baboon dropped to all fours. With a last look at Kessler he turned away, farting loudly as he did so. Kessler burst out laughing and, raising himself in the saddle, he forced a similar response.

"You too, old man," he called, still laughing. "Come on, Kaiser. Let's go."

At Khorixas, the halfway point of his trek, Kessler stopped at a wilderness farm. He stayed long enough for a home cooked meal and a good sleep.

"How was the trek, Franz?"

"I lost five cows on the way. Bloody scavengers. But I got my revenge. Three lions attacked me at night near the Hoanib River and I got all three," Kessler waved his fork in the air as he chewed on a thick steak and told his story at the same time.

"Now you are going to Windhoek to see de Groot?"

"Ja, they are mostly his cattle."

"Two of my boys are taking a small herd to Windhoek also," the farmer said. "You can all trek together for safety.

Though Kessler was getting desperate to tell someone about his diamond, he kept quiet. Suddenly he trusted no one, not even his friends. He vowed to say nothing until after he had sold the gemstone.

Eighteen days after he bought the diamond, in an early afternoon of late October 1936, following a gruelling desert ride of nearly six hundred kilometres, Kessler handed over the cattle to the herd's owner. With his pay in his pocket, he walked through Windhoek: a man on a mission. Ignoring the few shops and other pedestrians, he turned off the main street and counted down the numbers on a dusty side road until he found what he was looking for. With a quick glance up at the faded wooden sign over the door, he walked into the office of Manfred Goldstein & Sons Diamond Company.

Manny Goldstein couldn't believe his eyes when his trail-weary visitor unfolded a dirty piece of cloth and laid the stone in front of him.

"My name is Kessler," he announced without preamble. "How much will you give me for this?"

Manny blinked to hide his initial shock. He placed his bony white hands on the desk, on either side of the stone without touching the soiled cloth.

"Where did you find it? When?"

"Up in the northern Namib, by the dunes not far from the Hoanib. An old Ovambo sold it to me about three weeks ago. How much will you pay me?"

"Give me a few moments to think. It's not every day I see something like this."

Manny screwed an optical glass into his right eye and poked it at the stone. Breathing heavily, he could only find one word as he peered at the treasure.

"Wunderbar. Wunderbar," he repeated, over and over again.

Kessler waited impatiently, never taking his eyes off his diamond. "How much, Mein Herr?"

"Sit down, Herr Kessler, over here," Manny motioned his visitor to an old stuffed leather armchair. "We need to talk for a while. I have many questions for you, as you have only one for me. Now, tell me, what were you doing up there in that hell of a wilderness?"

"I was bringing a small herd of cattle down from the Cunene River for old man de Groot," Kessler answered. "I go there once each year. I like it there. It's very beautiful."

"Hmm. Sounds hot to me," Manny muttered, then, "Tell me more."

Slowly and carefully Manfred drew the story from the young cattleman. For much of the time he listened in silence, only prompting with a short question when an obvious gap appeared in the tale. He was a good audience. He gasped in horror when he heard about the attack by the pride of lions, and he grunted and furrowed his brow in surprise when Kessler told him of the lowly price he had paid for the stone.

"Young man, that's almost obscene. Don't you have any idea how much your diamond is worth?"

Kessler looked embarrassed and shook his head. "No, Herr Goldstein, only that it must be a lot of money."

"Let me tell you a story for a moment, only a short one. Perhaps then you will understand a little more about this...," Manny hesitated a second, "...this incredible stone."

He moved his chair closer and leaned forward, his elbows on his bony knees. Locking his fingers together he tapped his own lips with extended forefingers.

"Back in 1869," he began, "down on the Orange River not far from Hopetown, a diamond was found. It was probably only the second diamond ever found in Africa and recognized as such by white men. That diamond, colourless, not blue like this one, weighed eighty-three point five carats."

Manny raised his eyebrows and smiled at Kessler. He reached to the table and picked up the rough stone in one hand.

"This uncut diamond, I suspect, weighs ten times that much and you only paid two cows for it." Manny shook his head and started to laugh. Kessler watched him warily, his eyes screaming his important question at the diamond merchant. Manny's thin laugh trailed off as he gradually regained his former composure.

"Two cows. Two cows only. Oh, dear me," he started to laugh again.

"Herr Goldstein?"

"I'm sorry, my boy," Manny blew his nose sharply into his handkerchief and wiped his eyes with the back of one hand. "Two cows," he said again, shaking his head in disbelief. "Two cows."

"How much, Herr Goldstein?"

"Ah yes. How much indeed?" Manny echoed. "Indulge me a moment. Let me finish my story."

For a moment he seemed about to start laughing again then, abruptly, Manny sat upright, a serious expression on his face.

"That diamond, back in 1869, earned the Griqua shepherd boy who found it a fortune in livestock. Not two cows, Herr Kessler. Not just two cows," he waved his hands in the air, standing up in his excitement and walking towards the door. He turned and continued his tale. "That boy was paid five hundred sheep, ten oxen, and a horse. And you got this magnificent stone for two cows."

Manny shook his head in wonder and walked back to his desk. "Two cows, he muttered. "Only two cows."

13

He wanted this stone so badly. He had already calculated in his mind how much he would have to pay for the pleasure of ownership. The shrewd diamond merchant was a past master at assessing the value of a gemstone. He knew, within a few pounds, what the rough diamond would fetch on the European market. Once processed its value would be astronomical. Reaching for a piece of paper and a pencil he wrote a figure and turned it to face Kessler. The cattleman went white. He touched the edge of the paper with the dirty broken nail of his right forefinger. Nervously he tapped the figure, his lips tightly compressed and a worried look on his face.

"Do you have so much money, Herr Goldstein? Do you have it here in Windhoek?"

"No, young man, I don't have it here. It's in Cape Town – in my bank. I will give you a receipt for the stone and a letter of credit. You take it to the bank and they will arrange transfer of funds from my account to yours, just the way you do it when you buy cattle."

Kessler didn't bother to tell him he had never seen so many zeros strung together in his life. He pursed his lips and studied the figure carefully, trying to imagine what so much money looked like. Finally he raised his eyes.

"Ja, okay. I will sell it."

Manny Goldstein wrote out a letter authorizing transfer of the agreed amount from his bank account to Kessler. Carefully he blotted the ink. To make sure it was dry he breathed on the letter, looking at Kessler over the edge of the paper.

"So, what will you do now, young man?" he asked as he handed the letter of credit over. "Will you go back north again?"

"Ja, Herr Goldstein, I will. But this time I can build my own farm and buy a herd of cattle for myself."

He stood up, folding the letter carefully and placed it in his shirt pocket. Hesitantly he reached out his gnarled fist and wrapped it in a suffocating grip around Manny's delicate hand.

"Danke, Herr Goldstein. Danke schoen," he spluttered earnestly. At the door he turned and repeated his thanks, a huge smile of delight working its way over his sun-creased features.

"Good luck, Herr Kessler. Good luck with your farm."

Goldstein locked the door behind Kessler's departing back and pulled down the window shades. Under the artificial light of a desk lamp he studied the newly purchased stone with renewed interest. As he turned it slowly he examined it with a professional's eye. For over an hour, talking to himself in whispers, he analyzed the diamond's true potential. At last, with a deep sigh, he turned off the light and sat in darkness. Holding the diamond tightly in his hands he began to weep tears of joy. After a lifetime of searching, he held a large, almost perfect diamond in his hands. Kessler was rich, or would be when the balance of the money was transferred to his account. Goldstein, already a reasonably affluent man, was suddenly extremely wealthy. Over dinner that night he showed the rough diamond to his wife, Esther, and their twenty-four-year-old twin sons, Benjamin and David.

"What is it worth, Papa?" asked Benjamin.

"How much did you pay for it?" David chimed in.

"I paid twenty thousand pounds. No more. No less," Manny told his sons smugly. "And it is worth perhaps closer to one hundred thousand. Once it is cut and polished it will be worth at least one million American dollars."

"Why American dollars, Papa? Why not sell it for Rand or Sterling?" David asked.

"Because I will sell it in America, that's where the real money is today."

"Is it so pure, Manny?" his wife broke in. "There may be flaws in it you haven't seen yet."

"It is almost perfect, I tell you. Look at its clarity. Look at its colour. Never was there a diamond as beautiful as this. Even the one they call the *Queen of Holland*, an intense blue stone I'm told, could not be as beautiful as this one. I must take this stone to Amsterdam myself to be cut and polished. I can't trust anyone else with such a priceless gem," Manny told his family. "You boys must look after the business and your mother while I'm gone."

"The next steamer leaves Cape Town in ten days, Papa. After a stop in Luderitz, it will be in Walvis Bay the next day," David said, "and it stops in Rotterdam en route to Hamburg. You can be there with Uncle Jacob in a month."

* * *

Franz Kessler stood smiling to himself on top of a broad knoll. It stood ten metres prouder than the surrounding land and appeared much higher than the horizon and the dunes to the west. He took off his sweat-stained hat and threw it in the air with excitement. All around him lay his newly acquired land. The deep red of the fertile earth contrasted sharply with the blue of the early morning sky. Soon the warm lowing of contented cattle would drift across his property. Soon, once he finished laying out the foundations, his own home, which he had designed himself, would grace the highest point of his own piece of Africa. Then, when all was ready, he would return to Windhoek or maybe go further – perhaps as far as Cape Town – to find a wife to give him strong sons. Smiling happily Kessler picked up his hat and dusted it off against his pants.

Kessler had chosen his land with care. Taking long confident strides he staked out the corners of his house. Then, far enough away to keep a dignified distance between them, and at a lower elevation, he marked a large rectangle for his cowhands' bunk house. Over there, near the main kraal to the south, a deep artesian well waited to supply fresh clean water. Until the main house was built he planned to sleep in a tent, near his cattle. His cowhands would build their own bunk house, then help him build his home. Already they were busy fencing the perimeter of his spread. Satisfied with the basic layout, Kessler prepared to join his men.

"Come, Kaiser," he called. "We go to work."

Kaiser obediently trotted towards him and nuzzled his hand affectionately. Kessler stroked Kaiser's noble brow, tracing the irregular outline of white above his nose. Long ears flicked a warning at a quartet of determined flies as Kaiser tossed his head.

Pushing forward he exhaled, breathing warmly into his master's ear. Kessler laughed and hugged the great head to him.

"We are rich, my Kaiser. All this is ours now."

Without effort, he vaulted into the saddle and turned away. He had a long ride to the boundary where the work was in progress. He was keen to get started on his farm. Responding to the slight pressure of his owner's heels, Kaiser settled into an easy trot. An hour or so would see them at the eastern fence.

Neither Kessler nor Kaiser saw the long, slim olive-coloured snake with black-rimmed eyes, until it was too late. Kaiser reared suddenly in alarm as the black mamba struck at its foreleg, narrowly missing its target. Kessler, deep in thought, still planning his future, was taken unawares. He fell heavily, banging his head on a sharp rock, as Kaiser twisted sideways in an effort to keep clear of the danger. Rider-less, the horse danced left and right, its front hooves thrashing the air. Stumbling backwards, its right hind hoof broke through into a springhare's burrow trapping one leg. Struggling to free itself the panic-stricken animal screamed and crashed to the ground. Stunned by his fall, Kessler put out one hand to steady himself as he tried to rise. His hand touched something smooth which moved under him. Dimly he heard Kaiser whinnying in pain. A sharp blow, like a stab from a knife, numbed his hand. Kessler rolled shakily to his feet, aware of the serpent slithering away to his right. He looked at the two punctures on the back of his hand in horror.

"Kaiser. Here Kaiser," he called as he staggered towards his mount.

Kaiser lay on his side, a broken bone sticking through the torn skin and bloody flesh of one hind leg. The horse snorted loudly, its chest heaving with pain and fear, its eyes rolling wildly.

"Oh no, not now," Kessler groaned as he knelt beside the doomed creature. "Not now."

He looked at his hand, which was swelling rapidly. Urgently he sucked at the wound, desperately trying to draw the poison. Spitting out contaminated blood, he took his knife and opened the wound more, hardly aware of the additional pain. Once again he sucked hard, knowing only too well it was of little use.

With a shake of his head he drew his rifle from the long, leather saddle holster. Fondly he knelt and kissed Kaiser on the bridge of his nose.

"Goodbye, old boy. Goodbye," he whispered, unbidden tears making him blink his eyes furiously.

Taking two paces back, standing ramrod straight, he held the rifle in his good left hand. Bracing the stock against his hip he aimed the barrel at Kaiser's brain. Steeling himself against the hurt in his mind and the agony building in his right hand, he fired once. The rifle slipped from his fingers as he stood with bowed head for a few seconds. Abruptly he turned on his heel. Without a backward glance, Kessler began to retrace their steps to the place where he had planned to live. Clasping his injured right hand with his healthy left, he walked with measured steps: left, right; left, right. The cadence as steady as a drum beat: as steady and mournful as a solo snare drummer leading a coffin to a graveyard. He placed one foot in front of the other on the rich, red earth, without looking down, without swaying. Always his gaze remained fixed on a distant rise. Already a red line, the thickness of a pencil, was creeping unchecked up the middle of his forearm: just as mercury in a thermometer would rise degree by degree on a scalding hot day.

The toxins, which had been force-fed into his vibrant young body by wickedly sharp teeth, were hard at work. Systematically they destroyed his flesh, attacked his nervous system; took away all hope. Although Kessler understood nothing of the scientific process breaking down the very fibres of his being, he accepted that death, his death, was imminent. He could have simply laid down where he was and saved his energy: saved it to, perhaps, gain a few more precious minutes of life. Kessler was too stubborn, too determined. Tucking his throbbing injured hand into his shirt he strode on, his pace never varying. Halfway between the carcass of his horse and the hill he faltered; stopped for a moment. His chin dropped and he gave a deep, rasping sigh. For a few seconds he stood there with his head bowed. Then, raising his head he took another big breath and forced his right foot forward again. If he was to die, then he would do it within the boundaries of his own homestead, not out on the veldt. He would die within the markers of the house he had planned to build. As he staggered up to top the rise, the highest point of land on his domain, his breathing was more ragged, his muscles weaker. Carefully he pulled a handmade cigarette from his shirt pocket, finding it difficult with one shaking hand. Striking a sulphur match on his boot, he held the flame close to his mouth. Taking a deep breath, he sucked the hot, blue smoke hungrily into his waiting lungs.

Once strong enough to carry him the length of his land without tiring, his legs lost their strength. His knees weakened and buckled. Kessler slumped to the ground, falling on his chest, his head to one side. Through rapidly failing eyes, his vision fading and partially clearing as erratically as the pounding of his pulse, he tried to focus on the ridge of knife-edged dunes cutting the horizon. Over there, where the real desert began, his life had changed irrevocably. The day he first held the diamond: a day like any other in the Namib. A day of unrelenting heat: a day of little movement.

Long before the hands rode in for the night the deadly, cloudy yellow venom took Kessler's life. The first riders found Kaiser where he had fallen. One of the riders dismounted to pick up Kessler's discarded Mannlicher rifle. A short time later they found their boss crumpled in a heap on the highest point of his land. His eyes were open, staring in sightless futility at the distant dunes.

Chapter 2

After a hot and dusty drive in an uncomfortable old bus from Windhoek, via Swakopmund, Manny arrived in Walvis Bay an hour before his ship sailed. As soon as he had checked in with the shipping agent, he made his way on board and went directly to his cabin. He did not feel well. The all-pervading stench of fish from the trawlers, the incessant screaming of the gulls, and the sight of the rolling ocean made Manfred Goldstein sick. After the clean, clear semi-desert air of Windhoek, the small, bustling sea port among the dunes did little to endear him to the coast.

Manny did not enjoy the voyage to Europe. He hadn't expected to. The unforgiving Skeleton Coast, graveyard of shipping from Swakopmund all the way north to the Cunene River, terrified him. He had no wish to see, or think about, the impossible barrier of gigantic sand dunes fortifying the land and battling the restless Atlantic Ocean. The sea itself was a power which dominated him totally. He had no understanding of its capricious moods and no interest in learning about it. Within minutes of casting off her moorings the ship began a steady roll. Manny started being seasick while the coastline of South West Africa was still in sight.

Thirty-one years before he had experienced the same distress on his outbound voyage to Cape Town. He had been twenty-one then. Determined to make his fortune, he had handled his disability bravely and survived the long voyage. The only difference on his return was that he had succeeded in his goal. He had made his fortune.

As the ship ploughed north across the ocean towards the equator, Manny spent much of the time in his cabin. Unlike him, his fellow passengers, German and Dutch for the most part, took advantage of the first half of the cruise to relax in the tropical sun. There would be time enough for them to stay inside when the ship crossed the equator and finally reached cold European waters.

Feeling a little better and in need of fresh air one morning, Manny ventured on deck and settled himself in a deck chair. A handful of other passengers sat talking a few chairs away. Next to Manny an elderly couple snored in unison. A child ran a toy car along the ship's wooden rail. There was no land in sight. The ocean stretched and rolled to infinity in all directions. The ship moved in concert with the waves, responding to their every whim, adopting their rhythm. The Atlantic reflected the deep blue of the tropical sky. Manny failed to notice the similarity in colour between the sea and his diamond. He tried not to look at either sky or water. Stoically he closed his eyes and tried to relax.

From the nearby group a German voice droned on about the political situation in Europe. Occasionally he was interrupted by a loud snort from one of the sleepers. Manny half listened to the conversation without taking much interest, until one comment made him forget the ship's motion.

"Deutschland and Japan will sign an alliance, just as we have signed an agreement with Mussolini's Italy," the voice proclaimed. "Together we will protect Europe from the combined menace of the Bolsheviks and the Jews."

"Herr Hitler has already begun work on the Jewish problem," another broke in. "He has taken away their German citizenship and barred them from public life. Soon we will take their businesses as well."

Manny listened with mounting horror as the conversation passed back and forth among the group. His stomach began to rebel again, a reaction to words and waves. With his hand over his mouth he rushed below to his cabin; and there he stayed for the remainder of the voyage.

When the S.S. *Kaiser Wilhelm I* finally docked in Rotterdam, November was almost over. After a rolling Atlantic voyage, an excruciatingly uncomfortable crossing of the Bay of Biscay and gales in the Channel, the ship was finally still. It was raining hard in the bustling Dutch sea port. While men scurried in the wet to begin unloading, the dock glistened in appreciation as it was washed clean. Low clouds swirled uneasily around the skeletal outlines of the dockyard cranes and beyond to soften the dramatic thrust of the cathedral's twin spires. Wearing the same raincoat he had worn when he left Rotterdam as a young man, Manny was the first passenger off the ship. Like many others, he was eager to have his feet firmly planted on stable land again.

Tucked under his arm, Manny clutched a scratched leather attaché case with his left hand; in the other he held a nondescript suitcase, also of faded leather.

"Manny, Manny, it's so good to see you again." Outside the customs' shed Goldstein was swept into a bear hug by his older brother, Jacob. "Come we must go home. Rachel is dying to meet you."

Jacob picked up Manny's suitcase and weighed it in his hand thoughtfully. "You travel light. That means you are not staying long I suppose?"

Manny nodded, "Not long, Jacob. Not long."

The two brothers, who hadn't seen each other since Manny sailed from Europe three decades before, hurried arm in arm through the rain to a waiting car. Manny still swayed a little, as if in anticipation of the sea beneath his feet.

In the unmoving comfort of Jacob's home, Manny told the story of the huge diamond. Enjoying himself immensely, he kept his audience waiting as he drew out the tale. Every word Kessler had told him about buying the diamond was engraved on his memory. Every word was repeated, with emphatic gestures, to his spell-bound brother and sister-in-law. At last he stopped. He took a sip of red wine and wiped his lips carefully with his handkerchief.

"And now...," he announced, standing before them proudly.

They watched as he removed a package from his attaché case. Slowly he unwrapped the contents until a large dull stone, looking like nothing more than a chunk of weather-worn blue glass or crystal, lay on the table. He looked down at it with misty blue eyes, his hands hovering protectively around it.

"Well, so there it is," he breathed.

Rachel was disappointed and it showed. "Are you sure you haven't made a mistake? It doesn't even sparkle."

Manny smiled. "No, Rachel. There's no mistake. This is one of the most magnificent diamonds ever to feel the touch of a man's hand." He stroked the stone lovingly.

"It's big all right, but it doesn't look like a diamond to me. It's more like a piece of coloured glass."

"Rachel, Rachel, all diamonds look like this before they are processed." Manny pointed to her hand, "Even your diamond, your beautiful engagement ring, once was rough and pitted like this one."

Rachel looked at her hand. She twisted her ring and held it up to the light. "That will sparkle like this one, when it is polished?"

"When this is cut and polished properly, I believe it will be the talk of the industry and the object of much competition. All the blue-bloods of Europe and America will be bidding for this one gem."

"You don't think the depression, here in Europe and in America, will affect the sale of such a diamond?" Jacob wondered.

"No, I don't. The wealthy always have money for investments such as this. Perhaps even more so now there is little confidence in the stock markets."

"What makes a diamond so valuable, Manny? How is one graded higher than another? Is it just size?" Rachel rolled the questions out as fast as they occurred to her.

"The four C's, Rachel," Manny answered. "The four C's. Carat, cut, clarity, and colour. You see, it is the combination of those specific characteristics in a variety of equations that determines the value of a diamond. Its weight is always measured in carats, a very small amount. One carat equals only one-fifth of a gram."

"What about the cut?" broke in Jacob. "How does that affect the value?"

"The diamond cutter's skill, or lack of it, can ruin or enhance any diamond. One mistake and instead of one big diamond worth a fortune, there are many little diamonds worth not so very much."

"You will need the finest craftsman in Europe to cut it exactly. Do you know who that is?" Jacob asked.

"There is a man in Amsterdam who is reputed to be the best, but he must be quite old by now. I will go there tomorrow. There is much to be done. I don't want to keep this stone in Europe any longer than I have to. I don't trust that arrogant little Austrian in Berlin."

"What about clarity and colour?" Rachel asked. "You didn't finish the story."

"Ah yes, clarity and colour," Manny rubbed his chin thoughtfully. "Basically, a perfect diamond has no flaws. In other words, light can pass through it effortlessly. That is its clarity."

"And colour. Why is colour so important?"

"Well, of course, colourless diamonds are worth a lot of money. They always have been. But coloured diamonds were not always so important. That changed in the seventeenth century when Tavernier, the jeweller to the court of Louis XIV, introduced coloured diamonds to the royal courts of Europe. He brought them from India. Only deep colours are valuable, Rachel. Deep colours like this one," Manny held up his diamond to show her. "Blue, pink, and purple earn the highest prices".

"How high are these prices, Manny?" Jacob asked.

"A blue diamond called the *Queen of Holland*, which weighed one hundred and thirty-six carats, was sold to an Indian Maharajah for one million dollars. And then there is the *Hope*, a dark blue diamond from India. In 1908, the Sultan of Turkey is said to have paid four hundred thousand dollars for it. Oh yes," Manny sighed, "the price will be high. It will be high."

The three sat talking about the diamond and about the possibility of war in Europe until close to midnight. Manny finally began to yawn between sentences, sometimes in the middle, and begged to be allowed to go to bed.

"Of course," Jacob replied, jumping to his feet. "You have been travelling for a long time, you must be tired."

* * *

In a dingy third floor apartment overlooking a narrow canal in Amsterdam, Hugo Van den Eynde studied the stone in front of him with a bemused expression on his face. At seventy-six his shoulders were hunched from a life spent leaning over a work bench. His knuckles were red and swollen with arthritis. Slowly he took the wire-framed spectacles off the bridge of his nose and polished them with the end of his tie. He shook his head once or twice, causing his silver hair to fall over his eyes. He brushed it back carelessly with one hand and looked up at Manny.

"How I wish I could help you. I never thought to see such a beauty. All my life I have worked with the most exquisite stones, but this...," he stopped and indicated the uncut diamond on his desk, "This is the most incredible gem I have ever seen. Few diamonds such as this have passed through Amsterdam."

Hugo rubbed his hands together gently and held them out to Manny, as if for inspection.

"These old hands have created masterpieces of the jeweller's art. Never did they let me down. They were so steady. No one could believe the feats we performed together. We could cleave a stone so perfectly. Never did we make the smallest mistake." He smiled in memory of his skills. "Now look at me. I can't even hold a coffee cup without my hands shaking."

"What do you recommend, Mijnheer Van den Eynde? Who can be trusted with my diamond?"

"You will have to go to Antwerp. Ask at the Antwerp Diamond Institute. Tell them you need to meet Piet de Kerpel. He is the best there is now."

Manfred Goldstein, a diamond dealer for all his adult life, had never been to Antwerp. Although he corresponded occasionally with a few members of the four diamond exchanges, he knew no one other than by name. From the lobby of a small hotel on Amsterdam's Keisergracht, he phoned a contact at the Diamond Institute who agreed to arrange a meeting with Piet de Kerpel the following day. Manny took the late afternoon train back to Rotterdam. Antwerp was less than two hours from there by rail. The morning would be soon enough.

As his train finally rattled and steamed its way over the points to the ancient Belgian city on the River Scheldt the next morning, Manny looked out of the window eagerly. The imposing facade of Beurs voor Diamanthandel, the second diamond exchange to have been opened in Antwerp, greeted him on the left. The gleaming gilded letters of the name were in sharp contrast to the leaden grey of the morning sky.

Below him, he knew, was Pelikaanstraat, the shop window of the jewellery trade. This was the centre of the diamond world. His world.

With a final belch of clag, which curled smokily upwards to add its pollution to the already blackened glass roof, the tired engine ground to a halt at the buffers. Scalding steam hissed in warning at passengers as the intense heat within the firebox kept the pressure high. Manny walked along the platform, edging away from the over-heated locomotive, looking up at the ornate clock as he went. The train was on time.

Descending the marble staircase into the main concourse, Manny looked around him with something approaching awe. The majestic building, created from the genius of a master architect's mind, did indeed look like the interior of a gothic cathedral, as he had once been told. There was nothing remotely so grandiose in Windhoek.

The diamond merchant, still firmly clutching his attaché case, mingled with the latest arrivals spilling out onto the street. He

27

looked briefly at the tree-lined avenue named de Keyserlei stretching before him, then at a piece of paper in his hand. Turning to his left he walked one block along Pelikaanstraat, peering with professional interest through the jewellery shop windows. A small sign, tacked on to a building on a corner, caught his eye. Manny crossed the road and peered up at the name. Nodding to himself with satisfaction, he moved away from the street of jewellery shops. A right turn took him into a narrow, cobblestone lane.

The buildings crowded together for company, each one part of the next, a shoulder touching a shoulder, a waist pressed against a waist. It was narrow and dark; the street in almost perpetual shade. As he walked, Manny looked up at the numbers. Finding the one he wanted, he rapped sharply with the iron door knocker shaped in the form of a lion's head. The door opened after a few moments to reveal a young man wearing the traditional ringlets of the Hasidic Jewry. Presenting his identity papers and a letter of introduction from Amsterdam, Manny waited politely until he was invited to enter.

Manny met Piet de Kerpel at his work bench after negotiating his way through three more guarded doors of the building. He was surprised, and a trifle concerned. Piet de Kerpel, master diamond cutter, looked far too young to be so skilled. He was, Manny thought, perhaps thirty-five at the most.

Manny's guess was out by one year. Though Piet de Kerpel was, at thirty-six, marginally older than he looked. His appearance was deceptive. When they shook hands, Manny discovered the diamond cutter's apparently soft hands disguised a grip of steel. His pale cheeks and boyish good looks hid the highly intelligent mind of a craftsman. Piet, perhaps the youngest skilled diamond cutter in the world, was the absolute master of his precise art. Manny took his cloth-wrapped diamond from the depths of his case. Carefully he peeled back the layers until the stone lay exposed to the light.

"May I?" asked Piet as he reached to touch the blue gem.

"Of course. Take it. You must get to know it properly."

Piet held the rough gem in one hand, turning it over and over with the other. He held it up to the light and smiled at its colour.

"You know how much it weighs, Mijnheer?"

"Yes, of course."

"We will see for ourselves." Piet weighed it, checking his brass scales carefully.

"One hundred and sixty-nine point two grams, Mijnheer Goldstein," he announced without expression. For a moment he was silent as he scribbled an equation on a pad of paper. "That's eight hundred and forty-six carats," he said, his voice betraying a slight lisp. The only sign of his interest was a slight sheen of perspiration on his forehead.

Manny agreed, his head bobbing energetically, "Yes, I know."

"I have never worked with such a large stone. Such a beautiful stone. This will take time to study. You understand?" Piet's eyes remained focused on the gem, "I need time to decide exactly how to cut it to the greatest advantage. I need a few days, at least, maybe more." He thought for a moment and then added, "Come back in two weeks, please."

Manny swallowed hard and nodded his agreement. "I will need a receipt of c-course," he stammered. Piet de Kerpel wrote the details of the diamond on a sheet of heavily embossed letterhead paper. He signed and dated it. Folding it once, he slipped it into a plain white envelope and handed it to the diamond's owner.

Manny spent the next fourteen days making contacts within the industry and fretting about his diamond. Until it was finally sold he would be a nervous wreck. He knew he could sell it in its rough state and earn a fortune. It was, after all, the third largest rough diamond ever found. Only the *Cullinan* and the *Great Mogul* were bigger. However, he was determined to wait until the processing was complete. Then, with a perfect stone, larger perhaps than even the famed *Koh-I-Noor* and, he suspected, a considerable number of smaller stones, he would earn many fortunes. Discreetly he set the wheels in motion to advise potential buyers that a fabulous blue diamond was soon to be available. When Manny returned to the diamond cutter's workshop on the appointed day, Piet was ready to show what he planned.

"Sit here, Mijnheer Goldstein. Sit here." Piet patted a high stool beside him. Manny did as he was told. On the bench, resting in the middle of a white cloth, was the large blue diamond.

"These are the cuts I propose to make. Here, here, here, and here," he pointed to the thin black lines drawn in Chinese ink. "There are not so many impurities to remove. The main stone will, I think, still weigh close to two hundred carats. It will be a magnificent diamond."

"And the stones cut from the original," Manny broke in. "Will there be many large ones?"

"Perhaps, if nothing goes wrong, there will be two more stones, maybe more," Piet paused a moment. "Maybe, one of forty or fifty carats and another close to the same. And many small but beautiful diamonds as well."

For a long quiet moment the two men appraised the diamond. Manny broke the silence. He cleared his throat and started to speak. A hoarse whisper escaped, nothing more. He cleared his throat again and blew his nose noisily into a linen handkerchief.

"When can you start?" he eventually managed to ask.

"I can start today, if that is your wish. It will take time as you know. The sooner I begin the better."

"Then I will leave you. I can be reached at this number when you need me."

Piet waited until Manny left; then he set to work. Mixing a small pot of quick drying cement, Piet positioned the heavy diamond on a wooden holder, or dop, with the grain running vertically. Held rigid in a special vice, the dop could not move in any direction. While he waited for the cement to harden he picked up a smaller dop. Glued to the top was a tiny diamond. He checked the sharpness with his thumb, without drawing blood. Satisfied, he tested the blue diamond's bond with the dop. It was solid. Carefully he scratched a fine groove along the ink line at the top of the blue stone with the small diamond. He was ready for the first cut.

The process Piet was about to undertake was not a new one. The technique of cleaving, or cutting diamonds, to remove impurities and imperfections, was known in India two thousand years before. Diamonds had been cut in Bruges and, later, in Antwerp, since the fifteenth century. Piet de Kerpel's father had been a diamond cutter, as had his grandfather and great grandfather before him. The art of cleaving diamonds had been born into Piet's brain and transmitted to his hands. Even so, he knew he would need all his skills to do justice to the incredible challenge in front of him.

Piet closed his eyes and made a deliberate sign of the cross on his head and chest. He knew of diamond cutters who had passed out with worry when cutting important stones. One man, considerably older than himself, had made a slight mistake and seen an expensive diamond shatter into thousands of minute pieces. He suffered a major heart attack and died a short time later. Piet had everyone reason to be concerned. The diamond in front of him was one of the most exotic stones in the world. One false move. One tiny error of judgement. That's all it would take to ruin it. Silently he prayed for a few minutes, his head bowed; eyes closed. His hands clasped together. Then, he opened his eyes and nodded his head.

"So, now, it begins," he muttered softly to himself.

He took a steel wedge, rounded rather than sharpened at the apex of the slim triangle. He fitted the edge in the slim groove on top of the diamond and held it there with his left hand. With his right he picked up a wooden mallet and held it poised over the wedge. Concentrating with all his might he raised the mallet a little. A sudden sharp blow on the wedge split the diamond in two, exactly along the fine black line he had drawn earlier. Piet put down his tools and wiped the sweat from his brow. He stood up from his stool, his head spinning, stars winking in his mind. The room rocked around him; everything was going black.

"Don't let me feint," he prayed, holding tightly to his work bench to keep from falling. He took a few deep breaths and

31

closed his eyes. Slowly he lowered himself until he was crouching on the floor. He bent forward and put his head between his legs, breathing deeply as he did so. Gradually his head began to clear. After a few seconds he was able to stand up without losing his balance. He took a sip of water and wiped his forehead again with a cloth. Peering into a small mirror he saw a ghostly white face staring back at him. Shaking with tension, he sat back on his stool and rested his head on the work bench. For five minutes he stayed that way with his eyes shut. When he felt better he straightened and picked up the two halves of the stone. With shaking hands he examined both pieces of almost pure diamond with a magnifying glass.

"Good. Good," he breathed.

Setting aside the smaller rough gem, Piet peered through his lens at the main stone. For a week he did no other work. For each of those seven days he worked on the rough, blue diamond. For each of his nights he prepared himself mentally for the following day's cutting process.

When he was at last finished with all his cuts the stones were handed on to the next expert. Each diamond had to be girdled, or have its base rounded, so that, more or less, it resembled the shape of a finished diamond. For the final part of the exacting task, they all had to be faceted on a polishing wheel. It was a long, time-consuming process. Each diamond, including the largest, would have fifty-seven facets, or plane surfaces. Most would feature the popular brilliant cut. The huge blue gem, softer in colour but larger than the *Great Blue Diamond*, or the *Hope* as it was more popularly known, would be a pendeloque - the shape of an inverted pear. It alone would be different.

While the diamonds were being processed in Antwerp, Manny tried, unsuccessfully, to wait patiently in Rotterdam. At least the enforced inactivity gave him and his brother much time to discuss the increasingly dangerous political situation in Europe. The British monarch's well publicized romance with an American divorcée had resulted in his abdication only days before. Edward's younger brother had already been proclaimed King in his place.

"We don't know where his sympathies lie," Jacob explained. "Edward wasn't King long enough to have much effect. This George the Sixth is an unknown quantity. But never forget, the family has a German background on one side."

"What about Hitler?" Manny asked. "He sounds dangerous and I believe he has ambitions to be sole dictator of Europe; at least."

"Ja, in Germany he is a problem. The Jews are being hounded out of business. Many have come to this country for safety."

"Is it safe here, do you think? On the ship I heard a German boasting about the Nazis' plans for Jews. It didn't sound healthy to me. And, I heard that Doctor Albert Einstein refused to stay in Europe more than a day or two in 1933. When he arrived in Antwerp by sea, he heard that Hitler had become Chancellor of Germany. Instead of continuing to Germany, he went straight back to New York."

"Yes, I know, but I don't think we have anything to worry about here in the Netherlands. We are a sovereign nation," Jacob argued. "The Nazi threat, if it is a threat, is unlikely to cross our border."

"I'm not convinced," Manny broke in again. "Only last year Hitler deprived all German Jews of their citizenships. Now they are merely subjects, with no rights. They are banned from all public life. And it will get worse, I'm sure of it. I want to get myself and my diamond as far away from Germany as possible. Einstein was right. And I think you and Rachel should leave too, with your children and their families."

Jacob refused to be talked into moving. "Rotterdam has always been my home as it was the home of our father and mother. I will not leave this city. What happens in Germany has nothing to do with the Netherlands."

"I hope you are right, Jacob," Manny closed the discussion, "but I wouldn't stay here."

Piet de Kerpel telephoned one afternoon. "Your stones are ready, Mijnheer Goldstein," he announced. "You may come tomorrow."

Manny spent most of that night wide awake. Alone in the single bed in absolute darkness, he watched a huge blue diamond drifting lazily across his universe. A new born planet. A new world for Manny. A string of distant blue stars kept station with the magnificent gem, each blinking its light in obeisance to a master.

Piet de Kerpel was not surprised to find Manny waiting for him when he arrived at work. Shaking hands warmly, the two made their way through the building to Piet's enclave. From a huge cast-iron safe, set deep into one wall, Piet took out a varnished wooden box. Placing it squarely on the table he lifted the lid and put it to one side. A white cloth obscured the contents. Manny leaned forward, peering through his glasses, trying to see through the opaque veil.

Piet dramatically unfolded the white cloth, corner by corner, with thumb and forefinger. Manny felt his chest constrict with anxiety. He needn't have worried. Nestled in the middle of a square cushion of soft white silk was his diamond. His first impression was of exquisite beauty. His second, a blink of an eye later, was that it was considerably smaller than the original.

"Where are the other stones you cut," he demanded of Piet, his anxiety making his tongue sound sharper than he intended.

"They are here, don't worry, Mijnheer, I haven't lost anything."

Manny flushed with embarrassment. "I, I'm sorry. I didn't mean to suggest..."

"I understand, Mijnheer. These are difficult times, and this is a beautiful piece of nature's work."

Piet opened one of two drawers at the bottom of the box and took out another identical cushion. On it, in the centre, were three diamonds cut in the brilliant style favoured by Antwerp craftsmen.

"You see, these three are also beautiful, are they not?"

He held up a velvet-covered tray. Sparkling like stars, a dozen or more small stones picked up the beam from the overhead light and scattered it around the room. "And these; not so bad either, eh, Mijnheer Goldstein?"

Manny picked up his magnificent blue diamond between thumb and forefinger. He held it up to the light, fascinated by the clarity of his gem. Goldstein's blue diamond flashed its icy brilliance back at its owner.

"It looks like it's on fire, with a million tiny blue flames," he murmured, "just like the night sky over the desert at home."

"It is more than twice the size of the *Star of South Africa*," Piet reminded him. "The same shape but a different colour."

"I will call it the *Namib Star*, Mijnheer de Kerpel. What do you think of that?"

"I think it is perfect. It shines like a star. I think it will be a star."

Chapter 3

Seven weeks and four days after he arrived in Rotterdam, Manny Goldstein sailed from Antwerp for New York on the small, old, passenger and cargo steamer *Ilsenstein*. Jacob and Rachel were there at the docks to see him depart.

"You must come to visit us in America once we are settled," Manny told them as they said their farewells. "I don't think I will ever go back to Africa now."

"Esther, she will join you in New York?" Rachel asked.

"Ja, if I can arrange immigration papers, she and the boys will make a new home in America. You should come too."

"No, Rotterdam is our home. And it's your home, too, here in Europe. Your roots are here. Surely, you will come back again?" asked Jacob.

"Maybe, one day. Right now I don't like Europe. It is increasingly being dominated by that fanatical Nazi in Germany," Manny's lips were tight, his eyes wrinkled, his face betraying his concern. "Europe is too dangerous for us Jews, including this one from Southern Africa; especially as I am a diamond merchant. I will not allow Herr Hitler to take my business from me."

A short time later the thick mooring lines were released fore and aft. Straining in unison, with thick black smoke belching from their funnels, two fussy tugs pulled the steamer away from the dock. Once out in the wide river and under her own power, the ship was set free to make her way down the placid Westerschelde to the open sea. For the first eighty kilometres, meandering between distant river banks, where wind and waves had little or no effect, the ship was steady. Manny hoped it would remain so but early January was not a good time to be on the North Sea, or the Atlantic Ocean.

Manny bore the rolling voyage down the English Channel reasonably well, managing to control his heaving stomach much of the time by thinking only of his diamond. After a few hours at Le Havre to pick up more passengers, *Ilsenstein* continued west. Once on the North Atlantic, where a winter storm built liquid mountains of green water to tower over the ship, even the thought of his diamonds couldn't protect him. Manny took to his cabin, suffering his seasickness in pitiful silence. There he stayed, in bed for all but a few hours each day.

The North Atlantic Ocean had no consideration for the puny ship crossing its waters, or for the passengers and crew on board. The ocean unleashed the full fury of its darkest winter mood on the ageing passenger ship, tossing it from giant wave to giant wave; rolling it carelessly from side to side and pitching it fore and aft. The days and nights dragged as the gallant vessel leaned into the battle and fought her way through. After what seemed an eternity of torment, a steward greeted Manny one morning with the welcome news that the storm had passed and the new world was in sight.

Manny washed and dressed. Protected from the winter winds by a woollen overcoat and scarf purchased in Antwerp, he put on his hat and went on deck to see America. Tucked under his arm was his old leather attaché case. Throughout the voyage it had been within arm's reach day after day. Even during his darkest hours of seasickness, it had never left his sight. He even took it to the bathroom with him. His precious, recently processed, *Namib Star* was, he believed, far too valuable to trust

38

to the safe in the purser's small office. Manny preferred to look after his own possessions. A potential buyer was already waiting in New York to appraise the gem. Three other blue diamonds, not as big but immensely valuable nonetheless, shared the journey. A packet of smaller gems, cut from the original stone, had been sold to an Antwerp dealer before he left Belgium.

As the ocean liner passed the Ambrose Channel Lightship, with Brooklyn just coming in sight to starboard, Manny and his fellow passengers lined the decks for their first glimpse of New York – their new world. Not until the Statue of Liberty came into view did most of them truly believe they had arrived. Manny smiled with pleasure, despite the cold wind and the threat of snow. He raised his hat to Lady Liberty and bowed his head for a second. Still ahead for the immigrants was the long process of immigration at Ellis Island. For Manny, arriving in First Class comfort as a business visitor, the disembarkation formalities were brief and the customs inspection minimal.

The first newspaper he read on arrival carried a short mention that the German Fuehrer and Reich Chancellor, Adolf Hitler, had guaranteed the neutrality of Belgium and the Netherlands.

"Thank God for that," Manny told himself, "Perhaps Jacob was right after all."

A few days after he arrived at the steamship terminal on Manhattan Island's south side, Manny hurried into the foyer of the Park Plaza Hotel. In a fifth-floor room overlooking Central Park, the newly cut and polished *Namib Star* changed hands. The sale was private, handled through an intermediary. The new owner preferred to remain anonymous, unknown even to the diamond dealer. Manny didn't really care whose money he received. Meeting the new owner was not important to him. The money was: it guaranteed his family's future.

As he handed over the glorious blue stone Manny spoke the traditional Yiddish words, "Mazel un b'rachah" - or, "Good luck and prosperity." The following day the buyer's bank authorized the deposit of one million dollars to Manny's credit.

He sold the three smaller gems to a jewellery design specialist a few days later and loaded his new bank account again. The jeweller showed Manny how he planned to set the three stones in triangular formation into a heavy gold necklace.

"They will sit here and I will offset their startling blue colour by a dozen clear diamonds. It will be a masterpiece, Mr. Goldstein."

The threat of imminent war in Europe and its inevitable worldwide repercussions set Manny on his next course, just as he had told his brother. With the help of distant relatives and aided by his wealth, Manny applied for and was granted American immigration status. He sent for Esther immediately, leaving Benjamin and David to sell the business in Windhoek. As soon as possible they too would set sail for America.

Manny Goldstein's concern that a war in Europe was inevitable was well founded. As 1937 and 1938 sped by the Nazi's were rarely out of the newspapers. Hitler made his homeland, the once independent Austria, a German province. He immediately set in motion a pogrom, which the Nazi newspapers dubbed 'the great spring cleaning,' to remove all Jews from professional stations. Oppression of Jews in Germany escalated. All Jewish property was confiscated. Threats, implied and real, against neighbouring nations became more frequent, although Hitler insisted he had no territorial claims in Europe.

On March 14, 1939, in spite of his vehement denials, Hitler and his storm troopers entered Prague and raised his standard over Hradzin Castle. Czechoslovakia had fallen without a fight. Five and a half months later the combined might of Germany's air and land forces invaded Poland. Britain and France declared war on Germany two days later. World War II had begun and six years of vicious conflict would change the world forever.

All the while war ravaged Europe, North Africa, the Pacific and south-east Asia, the *Namib Star* stayed protected in darkness in an underground vault in a New York City bank. Its owner didn't need to look at it to appreciate its value. Its beauty meant nothing to him. His wife would never have the opportunity of wearing it. An investment, the diamond was his protection against a second Wall Street collapse, no more, no less.

In 1950, five years after the war ended and now sixty-six years old, Manny Goldstein was no longer active in the diamond trade. On his sixty-second birthday, a stroke had left him speechless and paralyzed down the left side of his body. Esther was convinced that the stroke was precipitated when Manny discovered his only brother, Jacob, and his entire family had died in a Nazi concentration camp called Auschwitz. Though more than half his body no longer reacted when ordered, his mind remained alert. Unable to look after himself properly for most of the time, Manny was confined to his mid-town apartment overlooking Central Park. Occasionally Esther or one of his sons would take him out in his wheelchair so he could sit in the park; listen to the birds and watch the people. Most days, though, were spent indoors, reading and being ministered to by his fussy but devoted Esther. An adjustable brass music stand, permanently stationed beside his favourite leather armchair, supported his daily newspaper. With an effort he could just manage to turn pages with his right hand.

Occasionally he thought of the *Namib Star*, though he had never considered finding out who owned it. To Manny, privacy was a God given right. Once, a few years before, he had been interviewed by a journalist who was writing a story about coloured diamonds. Manny had been delighted to tell him all he knew about the precious diamond. But he couldn't give the name of the current owner.

He was surprised one day to read that his diamond, he still thought of it as his, had been sold again. The purchaser, one of six high-profile owners of West Coast Cinematography and a noted movie director, was pictured on the front page of the New York Times holding the *Namib Star*. "Movie Moghul Buys Diamond for a $Million," the headline shouted. The text, running two full columns, revealed at last the identity of the mysterious previous owner.

"Oil tycoon Carl Macaulay," the reporter wrote, "who purchased the striking blue diamond from South African dealer Manfred Goldstein before the war, suffered a fatal heart attack while taking a bath last year."

41

Manny had never heard the name, although he recognized the man's wide-ranging oil exploration business well enough. The story went on to add that the Oklahoman's wife, who was childless, had decided to sell the diamond for exactly the amount her husband had paid for it.

"I think it is an unlucky stone," she explained. "Everyone who has owned or come in contact with this diamond has suffered."

There followed a list, headed by Franz Kessler. He, the story said, died from the effects of a snake bite in the Namib Desert in late 1936.

Manny blinked in surprise at that, remembering the tall, gaunt young cattleman with something approaching affection. He wondered how the reporter had come across such an obscure piece of news. Even though he had given Kessler's name to a journalist some time before, he had never expected the man to follow up such a long-distance contact.

"Piet de Kerpel," the article read, "the man who originally cut the rough diamond, lost his right arm in an automobile accident." The story went on to say de Kerpel had been knocked down by a German army truck on May 27, 1940, the day before Belgium surrendered to the Nazi invaders who had promised the nation its sovereignty. De Kerpel was crossing an Antwerp street to go to work at the time. Manny's gentle blue eyes misted over as he read of de Kerpel and, immediately after, of his own misfortune. "Manfred Goldstein suffered a debilitating stroke in 1946 and needs constant care...Carl Macaulay, the last owner, was dead of a heart attack."

"I'm not superstitious," announced new owner Richard Campbell, "I don't believe in luck, good or bad."

"Who'd you buy it for?" screamed the press. "What's her name?"

"It's just an investment, guys. Call it life insurance if you like," the three times married Campbell was reported to have explained.

Manny leaned back against his cushioned chair and closed his tear-filled eyes. Esther came in as the tears escaped and trickled

42

down his pale cheeks.

"What's the matter, Manny, why are you crying so?" she asked, pulling him upright and fluffing his cushion. Manny hesitantly raised his hand part way and pointed to the newspaper. Esther frowned at the headline then rapidly scanned the story.

"Don't worry about those things, Manny, it's not so important now," she lectured him. "We have a good life here in America and that diamond made us rich."

Esther nodded wisely to herself as she scooped up the paper, folded it and put it out of her husband's reach. She patted him on the arm. "You sleep for a while now. You need more rest."

Manny leaned back in his chair and closed his eyes. He felt tired, needing more rest as Esther had said. As he drifted into sleep he saw Franz Kessler riding hard across the Namib Desert, silhouetted by the setting sun. In his hand Kessler held the *Namib Star*, holding it aloft so the sun's rays could scatter the brilliance over the land. It was the last image to cross Manny's mind. When Esther came in to see him later, she found him with eyes closed, head tilted back and slightly to one side. He was smiling. In death, his kindly old face was serene and peaceful.

BOOK 2

Hollywood, 1950

Chapter 4

Sandy Anders waited patiently with the remaining seven out of fifteen would-be actresses. Advised to be at the Hollywood studio by 8:30 a.m. she had been the second to arrive. Each clutched a portfolio of photographs, resumés, references and, in some cases, promotional flyers. For nearly three hours the nervous girls had sat in a sparse ante-room of almost bare white walls watching each other, comparing, mentally criticizing; making each other more and more uncomfortable. The hands on the old wall clock ticked slowly in circles. The girls were restless, wishing the minutes to pass; afraid of what was to come.

"Jessie Peters," a harsh nicotine-ravaged voice issued from beyond the door to the future.

All the girls sat up straight, checking their makeup for the hundredth time. A leggy redhead stood, smoothed down her faux leather skirt and strutted on stiletto heels towards the voice. Twenty minutes later another girl was called. From then on, at intervals of precisely twenty minutes, another name rasped from unseen lips. By one o'clock Sandy was hungry, her stomach grumbling unashamedly.

"Here, doll," the girl beside her opened her purse and held out a packet of mints, "chew on a couple of these, it'll settle your stomach."

Gratefully Sandy took two and popped them in her mouth. "Thanks...," she started to say.

"Sandy Anders."

"Oh, shit." Embarrassed, Sandy spat the uneaten tablets into her hand. A chorus of giggles erupted as she looked around for some way of disposing of the mess.

"Here, doll," a tissue held out by the same girl. "Use this."

Sandy nodded her thanks, wiped her hand and, without thinking, handed the used tissue back to the girl.

"Thanks, doll," she heard as the crumpled tissue, weighted by mints, soared across the room to rebound off a wall and drop perfectly into a waste bin in a corner.

On the other side of the door a smartly dressed woman, rather attractive, Sandy thought, held out a sheaf of paper. On the desk a lighted cigarette rolled off an over-full ashtray and lay smouldering on a notebook.

"Take these with you. Through there," the gruff voice, surprisingly masculine, was accompanied by a nod of the head and a bored look. Sandy walked through another door to find herself in a large well-lighted office. A distinguished looking man with silver grey hair and a proud Roman nose sat behind a rosewood desk. Sandy had time to register the expensive grey silk suit and the hooded eyes before a voice stopped her.

"Come in, stand there, in the middle of the carpet," a deep strong voice ordered. "Right, let's see what you can do."

Twenty minutes later, after reading a few pages of script, Sandy was outside the studio again. She had no idea what she had just read, or whether she had impressed or annoyed the man. He simply listened to her, watching her carefully, asked her a question or two; then politely thanked her in dismissal. She hadn't even been told his name or his position with the studio. That mattered little. Sandy had recognized Robert Cochrane immediately. The most respected producer in Hollywood was a Scotsman with impeccable taste in all things. She knew he was meticulous in casting each character in his films. Rumour had it he also insisted on screwing the pick of the crop before giving them a part. Sandy was vaguely disappointed that Cochrane hadn't said anything remotely lecherous. Not that she would have responded or accepted any sexual advances, she told herself.

Sandy Anders, born in Kalispell, Montana, of good Swedish stock, was the youngest of four daughters. At twenty-one she was convinced she had what it takes to become a star. With one minor beauty contest title in hand, she had arrived in Hollywood only a few weeks before. She was one of the thousands of hopeful unknowns who arrived by bus and expected to leave by limousine. Sandy, however, was different from many of the star struck arrivals; she had something special. Her looks were combined with a shrewd intelligence. The looks were her ticket through difficult doors. Her intelligence would do the rest. Sandy was smart and ambitious: extremely ambitious. She was a high school graduate clever enough to understand her own limitations, to know her expectations, and to exploit the beautifully proportioned assets nature had bestowed on her. The vital statistics listed in her resumé said she was only five feet four inches tall. Sandy made up for her lack of stature by wearing the highest heels she could find. Careful application of makeup emphasized the contrast between her natural flaxen hair and deep blue eyes.

Since leaving school at eighteen she had worked hard for a lawyer and saved most of what she earned. Her bank balance was comfortable enough to keep her clothed, housed and fed for up to one year while she looked for work in the show business world. Even though she had little acting experience, she didn't anticipate waiting that long for success. If others could learn, she could do the same. Deep down, she suspected, or hoped, that she would prove better than some starlets already featured on billboards. As insurance, Sandy took a job waiting tables for the breakfast crowd in Santa Monica, close to her small studio apartment. Her looks would, she determined, get her a few screen tests. Her intelligence, she promised herself, would keep her from the reported sweaty bounces on the casting couch. With only one less than satisfying sexual experience behind her, Sandy was not prepared to give quite everything away to realize her dream.

One week after her audition, as Sandy returned home in mid-morning from serving half-awake customers since daybreak, the phone rang. Dropping her keys and her purse on a chair she leapt for the phone, leaving the front door open.

"Hello, Sandy Anders speaking," she answered as calmly as possible.

"Miss Anders," a harsh well-remembered voice growled at her, "Can you meet Mr. Cochrane at the Beverley Hills Hotel for lunch at one thirty today?"

"Yes," Sandy answered, feeling the damp warmth of perspiration enveloping her body, "Yes, I'll be there. Thank you."

Sandy put down the phone, her eyes wide with excitement. "I've done it," she cried, shaking her head in surprise. "I've done it. I'm on my way."

She danced around the room with a cushion in her arms, singing to herself a simple refrain, "I'm gonna be a star. I'm gonna be a star. I'm gonna be a star."

Sandy spent the rest of her morning trying on clothes, deciding what to wear to the most important meeting of her life. She finally settled on a plain white dress with short sleeves, decorated with a wide red belt and identical coloured high heels. When she stepped off her bus on Sunset Boulevard, not far from her destination, her excitement became tempered by nerves. She walked slowly towards the palm trees decorating the grounds of the great pink palace where her future would be decided. For a long time she stood on the sidewalk near the entrance, watching the expensive cars and limousines coming and going. Finally, taking a deep breath, she checked her wristwatch a last time, straightened her back and stepped into the lobby of the hotel with all the confidence she could muster.

Cochrane was already seated at a corner table when Sandy walked into the restaurant, right on time. They shook hands

48

briefly and Cochrane motioned her to sit. Without a word, he signalled a waiter to pour champagne into two frosted glasses.

"Hello, Rob. How are you?" a voice drawled from close by. Sandy looked up at a stocky, deeply tanned, rather handsome man in his early forties. Casually dressed, he radiated confidence and warmth. Bold brown eyes, set under dark wavy hair, roamed over her as he stretched out an arm to shake Cochrane's hand.

"Hi, Rich, I need to talk to you later. Meet Sandy Anders. Sandy, this is Rich Campbell. He's directing my next big budget movie."

Campbell took her hand and managed to caress it, shake it, and let it go in one motion. He smiled at her encouragingly, in a friendly manner.

"Okay, Rob, I'll call your office this afternoon. Bye, Miss Anders, a pleasure to meet you."

"Make it tomorrow morning, Rich. I've got meetings all afternoon today."

It took exactly one and a half hours for Cochrane to overwhelm Sandy. She soon learned that the lunch meeting was nothing more than an excuse to spend a free afternoon with her. Later she decided that the day had been like riding a carousel at high speed, with no way off. By late afternoon, with more than half a bottle of Champagne inside her, she was lying on Cochrane's bed while he methodically and smoothly stripped her clothes from her. She couldn't have stopped him if she'd wanted to. All her good intentions drifted back to Montana on the wind as she began to understand the available shortcuts to potential stardom.

Later, bathed in sweat, they lay side by side on the bed, Cochrane smoking a cigarette. There were no words between them until the phone on a bedside table rang.

"That was great, kid," Cochrane grunted as he reached to answer it. "You're fucking great. I'll see you later. Now go take a shower or something for a while, I'm busy, sweetheart."

Twice that night, between phone calls, Cochrane decided Sandy was irresistible. Twice he took her, once on the thick pile carpet in his study, once more in the bedroom. Finally sated, he

49

lay back against a large pillow, smoking a cigarette and occasionally sipping on a brandy. Sandy curled up beside him, one leg over his and her head on his chest.

"You're okay, Sandy," Cochrane said softly. "I'll tell Campbell to set up a test for you tomorrow. If you're any good, the part's yours."

"Will I see you again?" Sandy asked, more into the thick hair on his chest than to him.

Cochrane groaned. "Oh, no. Maybe. Who knows. My wife's due back from Palm Springs tomorrow. I'll see if I can make time someday next week."

Sandy slid off the bed and stood up. She looked down at Cochrane's naked body with her blue eyes blazing. He sipped on his drink, took a pull on the cigarette, and blew a perfect smoke ring towards her.

"You're a real bastard, aren't you, Robert Cochrane? A real bastard. Don't forget to talk to Campbell, or I'll be back." With that Sandy started dressing. Cochrane watched with an amused expression on his face.

"If you've nothing better to do than stare at my body, perhaps you'd be good enough to call a cab for me," she said through gritted teeth. Cochrane dialed and gave the order as she had requested, never taking his eyes off her.

Cochrane never did call again. It wasn't his style. One broad, one day, was his motto. With a never-ending stream of lovelies knocking on his door, there was no time for more than a one-night stand with any of them, unless they were exceptional. True to his word, and somewhat to her surprise, he did recommend Sandy to Rich Campbell. The director agreed to the test.

Sandy did not shine as an actress. She did, however, have a magnetic appeal which, combined with her stunning looks, persuaded Campbell to give her a small part.

"It's only a walk-on and a couple of lines," he explained, "but it will get you noticed."

Campbell was right. The film did get Sandy noticed, but mostly by the director. The one day Sandy was on the set for her short stint almost drove the director crazy. Most of the day he

50

had an erection. Most of the crew knew it too. No one was in much doubt about the outcome of the day. Campbell took Sandy home and she skillfully put the lessons learned from Cochrane to good use. Even though her role in the film was finished, Campbell gave her a pass to visit the set each day so, he told her, she could learn from the other actors. By the time filming was completed a few weeks later, Campbell couldn't stay away from Sandy. The two had become inseparable.

No more than a month after the wrap party at the end of filming, tabloids all over the country proudly unrolled banner headlines proclaiming the *Namib Star* had been given to an up and coming starlet. The photograph showed a smiling blonde in a low-cut dress. Nestled in her ample cleavage was a huge diamond.

"Bigger than the Hope and more dangerous" announced many papers. "Sandy's Hope Chest" quipped one caption. "Sandy's Dangerous Diamond" reported another. One California edition simply and cheekily labelled the photograph, 'The Treasure Chest." A sub heading alluded to a potential Pandora's box.

"Rich Campbell to marry his diamond gal," sang the tabloids a few days on.

The gossip around Hollywood, the polite versions, said that Campbell's new wife had employed judicious cunning, combined with energetic use of her superb body, to snare one of Hollywood's greats. The story was not so far from the truth. Sandy entered marriage endowed with beauty, above average intelligence, a fabulous diamond, and a five-year movie contract. Though she soon heard the talk, like her famous husband, Sandy cared little for gossip and even less for fanciful stories about unlucky diamonds.

Campbell coached Sandy as only a brilliant director could. Even so it was an uphill battle. In the first year of marriage she appeared in small roles in four films. None of her limited speaking parts showed her to have any great theatrical promise. Her limited talent was adequate, no more than that. Campbell, hopelessly in love or, perhaps more accurately, in lust, persevered anyway.

"What are you reading?" Sandy asked Rich one night as he sat engrossed in a screenplay.

"Ann's Cottage, that's the working title," he replied looking up. "It's about Shakespeare and Ann Hathaway."

"Is it any good?"

"Hell, yes," Rich grinned, "written by the Bard himself and adapted by Todd Greenaway, the best screenwriter in the business. What could be better?"

"Who's going to star in it? I'm sure you already have some ideas."

"I'd like to get Niven, but he's committed for the next couple of years. Second choice is Edmund Sterling, if the money people agree. He'd be perfect with that voice and that classy accent."

Sandy thought for a moment. "Sterling is a great choice. Better than Niven, I think. What about Ann, who's top of your list there?"

"I can't tell you yet, Cochrane's being difficult on that one – he's bankrolling the film so he wants final say – but he'll come around eventually," Rich confided.

"I'd like to read it if you don't mind, when you've finished with it."

"Sure, you can have it tomorrow. I'm out all day."

In Rich's absence, Sandy studied the manuscript for a full ten hours. Practicing in front of a mirror, she forced herself to become Ann Hathaway. The English accent gave her trouble but she knew she could get coaching on that. As for the acting, the theatrical Elizabethan gestures she employed might have been appropriate for a member of the sixteenth century Royal court; they certainly did not suit the daughter of a Warwickshire farmer from the same period.

Rich came home late in the evening, after too many drinks, to be confronted by a wife spouting pure Shakespeare.

"What the hell do you think you're doing?" he asked, pouring himself a stiff bourbon.

"I can play Ann Hathaway, darling. I know I can."

"Forget it," laughed Rich. "It's a big role. Much too big for you. Cochrane would never agree."

Sandy worked on Rich for days, using every skill she possessed, physical and mental. Gradually she wore him down to the point where he discussed the idea with Cochrane. To his surprise, Cochrane thought Sandy would look good as Ann Hathaway. Sandy got the part. Edmund Sterling had already signed a contract as male lead. When he heard the news his reaction was typical of his well-known pomposity.

"Who? Oh, Campbell's tart. Oh well, at least she'll make me look even better than I usually do."

Expected to become Campbell's finest work to date, the film became his worst nightmare. Sandy knew her lines perfectly; not once did she stumble or fluff a word. Unfortunately, that was the extent of her talent. Her acting was wooden most of the time, almost puppet-like. Only occasionally did she look comfortable through the lens. Her co-star sneered from off camera each time she performed. When he missed a line, as he did from time to time, he immediately asking politely for a retake. Sandy bitchily added up his mistakes and reminded him whenever he made a comment about her. Rich tried, without success, to keep the peace. The two actors fought constantly, with each other and with the director.

As a screen couple, the two stars were perfectly matched in looks. Sterling, one of the most handsome men in Hollywood, played the Bard immaculately. Sandy, as Ann Hathaway, looked gorgeous. Her character, however, was barely believable. Inevitably she suffered dreadfully at the hands of the editors in the cutting room. Campbell and his technicians worked round the clock to salvage their epic. Sandy's part having been drastically reduced, Sterling's had to be increased. He insisted on an increase in his fee. The film ran over time and over budget. No matter what magic the dedicated technicians worked on the celluloid, it was not enough.

At one point Campbell threatened to junk the film. Cochrane and the other partners refused to allow such extravagance. They had more faith in Campbell than he had in his movie. Finally he gave in and agreed to release the epic, flawed as he knew it was.

On opening night, in front of a gala crowd, Campbell put on a brave face as he listened to the sniggers building around him in the darkened theatre. Sandy chewed on the corner of a white handkerchief, embarrassment causing beads of perspiration to break out all over her body. She couldn't look at her husband. He sat rigidly beside her, watching his career tumble. There was no doubt in his mind that his film would be savaged by the critics. A disaster at the box office was inevitable. Halfway through, unable to bear the expectation of outright laughter any longer, he dug Sandy in the ribs with his elbow. She looked at him sharply.

"Let's go," he ordered, stalking angrily from the theatre.

At home Campbell got out of his limousine before it completely stopped, leaving Sandy to follow, and stormed into their mansion. White with fury he poured himself a large measure of bourbon and drank it straight down.

"Aren't you going to offer me one?" Sandy asked, watching her husband cautiously.

"Get your own," he snarled. "You are an absolute disaster. I have never been so fucking humiliated in my life."

He poured himself another large drink and downed it in one swallow. With the empty glass in his trembling hand he pointed at Sandy. "You can't act. Tomorrow the critics will tell you that on the front pages, right after they've finished murdering me and my career."

"Don't be so melodramatic, darling," Sandy purred. "It wasn't that bad."

"Wasn't that bad? Wasn't that bad?" Campbell screamed at her. "It was fucking well terrible."

"If it was so bad, why did you release it?" Sandy spat back at him, "You must have seen something in it."

"Yeah. Your boobs and your butt. That's about all."

"You bastard," Sandy shouted. "Your brains are in your goddam pants."

Campbell drew back his arm and hurled his empty glass at Sandy, catching her on the shoulder.

"Feel better now," she taunted. "Why don't you throw a punch at me as well?"

Campbell didn't wait for another invitation. He bounded across the room and tore open a drawer to his desk.

"See this," he held up an envelope. "This is your contract. And this is what I think of it."

Sandy watched in silence as he tore the paper to shreds. "That contract has a few years to run yet, my dear. I'll sue you for that."

"You'll sue me," Campbell spluttered. "You'll sue me. I'll give you something to sue me for."

With that he slapped her hard across the face. Sandy's head snapped sideways and when she looked back her eyes were on fire. She aimed a kick at his groin, which he easily avoided. Before she could recover her balance, he grabbed her by the shoulders and shook her violently. Sandy broke free and ran for the door. Campbell caught her and spun her round. Swinging wildly he threw the punch she had been expecting. Sandy almost avoided it, but not quite. He caught her a glancing blow above her left eye before his fist slammed into the door frame. He heard and felt his wrist break as Sandy fell to the floor unconscious. The foundations of a marriage built on looks crumbled, as quickly as a career built on little else had faded.

By the time Sandy staggered up out of her daze her husband was gone. Holding one hand over her swollen eye she went to Campbell's study. With practiced fingers she opened the wall safe and removed a rectangular box covered in dark blue velvet cloth. Slipping the gold-plated catch, she opened the lid to reveal her diamond nestling in white silk. Instinctively she kissed it before closing the lid. She held the box in one hand and re-locked the safe. Sandy stayed in the house long enough to tidy up her eye with makeup, put on dark glasses, and pack a few necessities. She placed the *Namib Star* in her purse. Unable to see well enough to drive at night, she phoned for a cab.

"Beverley Hills Hotel, please," she ordered the driver.

Tango Perez, twenty-two-year-old polo player and playboy son of a Costa Rican banana plantation owner, checked into the hotel beside Sandy Anders. He didn't recognize her. She was only vaguely aware of his presence at the counter. She heard the clerk use his name but it meant nothing to her. Tango didn't care who she was, it was her face and her figure which attracted him. The rather obvious black eye was an added curiosity. He listened carefully as the desk clerk spoke to her.

"There you are, Miss Anders, number four-six-two. Andre will show you to your room."

Perez watched approvingly as Sandy's hips swayed to the elevator. Behind him the desk clerk waited patiently until the elevator door closed.

"Your usual suite is ready, Mr. Perez." He signalled to a bell boy to take the two hand-tooled leather bags. "Enjoy your stay, Mr. Perez."

"Thanks. I think I will."

Perez learned more of the identity of the mystery woman in the *Los Angeles Times* the following morning. As Campbell had predicted, the film critics delivered a scathing attack against Sandy and against him. The only high point listed among the paragraphs, otherwise devoid of praise, was that Edmund Sterling had acquitted himself extraordinarily well, especially in view of the incompetence of the director and the total lack of talent seen in his co-star. One critic, with a ferocity unparalleled in a review, publicly asked Rich Campbell at the end of his column if he still felt the *Namib Star* had been a good investment. To add insult to professional injury, the photo editor completed the brutal attack by pasting a picture of Sandy wearing the diamond round her neck. Sandy Anders achieved instant notoriety instead of the fame she craved.

Tango still had to wait three full days before he saw Sandy again. She got into the elevator at the fourth floor, planning to go for a walk, and stood almost close enough for him to touch her.

"Good afternoon, Senorita Anders, you're looking very lovely today."

Sandy looked up through her sunglasses at the grinning face beside her. Her mind registered certain undeniable facts, medium height, dark, handsome, and obviously rich.

"Thank you," she replied instinctively to the compliment, "Do I know you?"

"Antonio Carlos Riviero y Perez," he bowed slightly without offering his hand. "My friends call me Tango. Will you join me for a drink?"

"Why do they call you Tango? Are you an actor, Mr. Perez?"

"Please, call me Tango," he gave Sandy a disarming smile. "No, I'm not an actor. I play polo, and I raise ponies."

"But why do they call you Tango?"

"Because when I'm playing polo I make my ponies dance for me. Perhaps one day you will come and watch me play."

At the lobby level, Perez took Sandy lightly by the elbow, "Come with me, Senorita, I will tell you my life story."

Despite herself, Sandy laughed. The Spanish accented English reminded her pleasantly of Desi Arnaz. Before she was fully aware, she was seated in the bar on plush leather sipping chilled champagne. Tango Perez was a charming and cultured companion. Skillfully he drew Sandy's story from her, all the while feeding her tantalizing anecdotes from his own privileged upbringing.

"Our family has been in Latin America since the late sixteen hundreds. My ancestors were Spanish noblemen who went to Cartagena first, in Colombia. My great-great-grandfather moved to Costa Rica because he saw the potential for owning more land. Now my father has banana plantations, and he grows coffee and sugar as well. Plus, we have many cattle and I have my ponies."

"Do you have any brothers or sisters?" Sandy found herself wanting to know more.

"I have one sister. She is married and lives in Madrid. My sainted mother died when I was a little boy. Now I live on my father's estate near San Jose."

"Did your father marry again?"

"No, he will never forget my mother. Never."

The late afternoon stretched into evening. Sandy accepted Tango's invitation to dinner, unable to tear herself away from the vibrant young man. Her mind, often at odds with her body, subtly calculated how to turn this unexpected friendship into something more lucrative. Tango playfully, apparently absentmindedly, occasionally stroked Sandy's bare arm during dinner. She did little to deter the attention.

"Are you trying to seduce me, Tango?" she asked, putting her hand on his to hold it still.

"Si. I can't help myself. I like all beautiful things, especially these things," dark eyes flashed with delight as he pantomimed a perfect female figure with his hands held over the table.

"You have so many beautiful curves, Sandy. You remind me of a wild mountain road, and I am a powerful Ferrari racing car without any brakes."

Sandy laughed, "Turn your motor off for a while, Tango, we haven't finished dinner yet."

Tango understood and prepared to play the game to the end. Seriously he asked, "Why did you leave your husband? I read the reviews of your film, they were not kind, but that is not enough to wreck a marriage, is it?"

With a wry laugh Sandy took off her glasses and showed Tango her discoloured eye.

"Does that explain it?" she asked. "The great director, Rich Campbell, on the occasion of his first flop, was not afraid to pass on the blame and punch his wife. That's it for me. Divorce is the next step and he can pay for it."

Tango saw a mental picture of Sandy on the front page of a magazine wearing the blue diamond round her neck. The same photograph which had been in many of the papers after the ill-fated premiere. Tango Perez never missed society gossip. He knew a great deal about Sandy and her husband. All of it learned since he had read the film review. He was fascinated by other people and other people's possessions. He was particularly fascinated by diamonds. He desperately wanted to own the *Namib Star.*

After dinner the two sat talking for another hour, occasionally tasting their Cognac. Sandy decided that she would probably share the Costa Rican's bed that night. She found she was looking forward to it.

"Maybe," she mused, "for more than one night."

Late in the evening Tango Perez signalled the waiter and signed his bill. Stretching out his perfectly manicured hand to Sandy he said confidently, "Now, it is the time."

He was a lean and hard-muscled young man, a legacy of his polo playing years. Sandy was soft, curvaceous, and warm. They made love smoothly, comfortably, and satisfyingly in his suite. Stretched out on the king size bed afterwards, Tango continued to stroke the silky creamy skin.

"What will you do now," Tango asked later as Sandy snuggled contentedly against him, "Will you go home to Montana?"

"Not a chance. I'm staying in California. I'll sell my jewellery and buy a house with a pool. Then I'll go into business for myself."

"Tell me about your diamond, the blue one."

Sandy sat up straight, a look of consternation on her face. She took his jaw in one hand. "What do you know about my diamond? What do you want?"

"Take it easy, Carissima. Take it easy. I told you, I love beautiful things. I collect them. Maybe I will buy your diamond."

Sandy stayed exactly where she was. "Are you serious?" She shook his jaw hard. "Are you serious?"

"Of course I am, now, let go before you break my chin."

Sandy relaxed a little while Tango rubbed his jaw. "You have strong hands my beauty. When can I see your diamond?"

"The *Namib Star* is in a safe place. It's in the bank. You can see it when I'm ready to show it, not before."

"And the papers of provenance, you have them? They are there too, yes?"

"Yes, Tango, everything is there. But I still haven't said I will sell it to you."

Sandy stayed awake the rest of the night praying Tango wasn't trying to con her in any way. She planned to phone a polo-loving

59

friend in the morning and ask a few pertinent questions about the man who had recently made love to her so passionately. Beside her, Tango was deep in his own thoughts. He wanted to hold that diamond, to feel it in his hand, so much.

Sandy's phone call, during which her informant almost drooled into the phone, told her one important fact: the only fact that was relevant as far as she was concerned: Tango was rich enough not to bed her for her money. The diamond would be safe. She agreed to have lunch that day, but in Santa Monica, not in Beverley Hills. Sandy wasn't ready to face the curious stares of the rich and famous just yet.

Promising to join Tango for dinner, Sandy took a taxi home to collect her car. Campbell was there, spread-eagled across a couch. He had a pristine white cast on his right arm which was cradled in a sling. Torn and crumpled newspapers were scattered around the room. Sandy had no need to wonder about them, she knew the words by heart. Campbell snored loudly as she walked through the mess. He was out cold. Drunk.

Sandy selected her car keys, cleared her closets of clothes, and left without a backward glance. Campbell's wine dark Rolls stood in the garage next to his white Cadillac. Sandy looked at them, pursing her lips thoughtfully. With a shake of her head she rejected the thought and opened the door to her Mercedes. Minutes later the electrically controlled gates closed behind her for the last time.

Lunch was a predictable bombardment of questions; mostly about her involvement with Tango.

"How did you meet Tango Perez? Sandy, he's a prince of a man. Great body. Great polo player. Impeccable credentials. And, my dear, he's terribly rich. I envy you. You must tell me. How did you meet him?"

Sandy told the story so skillfully that, mercifully, she was spared a post mortem on the opening night disaster. Having explained that she and Rich had separated, and shown the discoloured eye, there was little more to be said. Stating the obvious was not part of her plan.

60

Sandy phoned her bank after lunch and made an appointment to open her safety deposit box that afternoon. She insisted on absolute privacy and an armed security guard outside the vault. The *Namib Star* was hers. Rich Campbell was not getting his hands on it again. She would show it to Tango; then put it away until the time and the price were right.

She phoned Tango from the bank, insisting he meet her there immediately if he wanted to see the diamond. He wasn't thrilled at being ordered to attend, but his curiosity overruled his annoyance. He arrived on time. If Tango was angered, or amused, at the security guard's presence he showed no sign. The perfect gentleman, he stood back, outside the vault, watched carefully by the guard, until Sandy called to him.

"Okay, Mr. Tango Perez, take a look at this."

Tango went in to find Sandy facing him under the cool glow of a single neon light. Round her neck she wore the *Namib Star* on a thin solid silver chain. The deep blue suited her. He thought it matched her eyes. Sandy lifted the pendant's chain over her head and handed the diamond to Tango. He took it almost reverently, holding it in the palm of his hand with his fingers bent protectively round it.

"Hold it up to the light, Tango. It's like a blue fire."

Tango did as he was told, sucking in his breath at the brilliance. No matter which way he turned it, the diamond flashed and sparkled, picking up the neon's rays and scattering them around the room. With a dignified nod of his head, he passed the diamond back to Sandy.

"Where are the papers?"

Sandy pointed to a sealed brown envelope on the table. "Open it if you want to."

Tango slit the envelope with his thumb nail, still looking at the diamond in Sandy's hand. Taking the papers out he leafed through them until he found what he was looking for: a certificate bearing the seal of the Antwerp diamond house where the *Namib Star* had been cut to its present size and shape in 1937.

"Bueno," he nodded, "Bueno, Sandy, we will go somewhere and talk."

BOOK 3

A Gathering of Thieves, 1990

Chapter 5   **New York State**

Ali Ben Rachid leaned idly against the door, an untouched can of cola in his hand, watching without being noticed as an intoxicated guy and a girl bent over the kitchen table trying, without much success, to open a bottle of red wine. April Young, wearing faded jeans and a shapeless brown sweater, watched from near the 'fridge. Too far gone to display any dexterity with their hands, the befuddled pair fumbled and giggled as he stabbed ineffectually at the cork with a corkscrew.

"I can't get it in," he belched softly, leering, and swaying towards the girl, "you'd better help me."

His partner giggled again and reached for his crotch.

"Not that one. The fuggin' corkscrew," he beamed at her, his eyes glazed. "I wanna drink first. I can't think without a fuggin' drink."

Letting go of the bottle the two collapsed against each other laughing in drunken gasps.

"I'm a fuggin' poet. D'ya know that?"

"Yeah. You're a poet and you do know it."

Ben watched as the two guffawed at their perceived wit. The guy nudged the bottle with his elbow. It fell on its side without breaking and rolled slowly towards the edge of the table. Ben leaned forward and caught it as it began its descent to the tiled floor.

"Careful, guys, we don't wanna waste good wine, do we?" Ben handed the bottle back with one hand as he lifted a wallet from a back pocket, quickly followed by a few folded bills from another.

"Open it f'me." The drunk thrust the bottle back into Ben's hand.

April straightened, took a step forward away from the refrigerator, her eyes open wide as the pick-pocket took the bottle. Just in time she put her hand over her mouth, stifling a gasp of surprise. Except for the bottle of wine, the pick-pocket's hands were empty. The thought flashed through her mind – What the hell did he do with the wallet and the money?

Ben opened the wine expertly while the two befuddled students tried to help. Placing the bottle upright on the table he winked at the guy. Leaning forward, one hand on the boy's lower back, he made a lewd comment in his ear, receiving the anticipated guffaw in return.

"Thanks, man. You can 'ave 'er after me."

Ben smiled his thanks and patted the girl on the rear as he left the kitchen. April followed still trying to work out how the thief had managed to make the wallet and the money vanish.

"What the fuck happened to my money?"

April and Ben spun round as one at the disgruntled voice. Beside them, propped against the arm of a couch, a short overweight teen peered into his wallet.

"I'm sure I had twenny bucks in there," he complained. Looking totally confused he felt the breast pockets of his fancy black and silver shirt.

"Nope. Whadid I do wi' it," he slurred, checking the pockets of his jeans again. "Where the fuck's my money gone?" Few, except Ben and April, heard him over the pulsating music and through their own mental fog.

"Dance with me. I'm serious," April forced a bleak smile at Ben and put out her arms as if to embrace him. Ben hesitated.

Slowly, through gritted teeth, April warned, "You'd better do as I say, and then get out of here real quick before you're caught. These guys will kill you."

Ben took her in his arms as he was told. She was half a head taller than he with a poor skin and mousy hair. He watched her cold grey eyes flickering nervously around the room, the dark lines underneath reflecting untold misery behind. Thin lips, held tightly together, had forgotten how to smile in happiness. Ben studied her curiously, his face close to hers. With more care, he thought, in spite of the dowdy appearance, she might have been pretty. She probably had been: once.

"What are you talking about?" he asked. "Who are you?"

"I'm April and I'm your new partner," she answered in a determined voice. "I think it's time to go, Sugar."

"What makes you think I need a partner?"

"You need me alright, you'll see. Right now you ain't got a choice." With that April led him out of the room, out of the house and into her life. "Which car is yours?" she asked. Ben indicated a red Mustang parked five cars away under a street light.

"That one. The Mustang."

As he unlocked the driver's door, April asked, "What's your name?"

"Ben. Ali Ben Rachid."

"Where we goin'? Where d'ya live, Ben?"

"I live in Syracuse. I'm at university near there. Cornell."

"How much did you score tonight?" April asked as they drove east on Highway 90.

"I haven't counted it yet, probably a couple of hundred dollars."

April whistled in approval, her mind racing. "That's great, man. It's better'n a real job."

She was silent for a while, deep in thought. Ben looked sideways at her. "What's the matter? You look worried."

April reached over and tugged at the back pocket of his jeans. "How did you get that guy's wallet back in his pocket? The one in the kitchen?"

Ben laughed, "Ah, that's easy. I just distracted him with the bottle and a few words. The girl hanging on to him did the rest. And I didn't put it back in his pocket. I put it in hers when I patted her bum as I left."

"But he'll think she stole it."

"That's her problem, not mine."

April raised her eyebrows briefly. "Man, you sure have a mean streak in you."

"It's all part of the game. Seeing how much I can get away with. You don't like it, you can walk from here." Ben moved to the inside lane and slowed.

"No, it's okay. I don't give a shit. Keep going for fuck's sake," April yelled in panic.

Ali Ben Rachid was twenty-five years old. The son of a doctor in Algiers, Ben had been sent to America at eighteen to complete his education.

"Algeria needs educated men, my son," the doctor reminded him. "When you come home you will have a choice of professions, unlike most boys your age."

Ben went to Cornell University in upstate New York to study English and politics. Although he was reserved, he proved popular with his tutors who appreciated his agile mind. Unfortunately for his family, Ben had no wish to return to Algeria for quite a few years, if ever. Ben thoroughly enjoyed his new life in America. In the land of the free he could do more or less as he wished. In Algeria he had been forced to obey his father and bow to religious fundamentalists in almost all matters. Although he was a reasonably good Muslim, Ben had no wish to live under the strict regime which, he was convinced, would eventually govern Algeria.

Dr. Rachid and his wife were proud of their eldest son's achievements in America. He was, they were told in his regular letters, teaching English part time at a school in Syracuse to gain more experience. The busy doctor told all his male patients about his boy.

66

"One day," he boasted, "my son, Ali Ben Rachid, will come home. With his education he will surely enter politics. He will be good for our country."

Ben let his parents believe he also taught Arabic at evening classes twice each week. The reality was far less inspiring. Ben's letters were, for the most part, deliberately deceptive. The truth would have broken the hard-working doctor's heart.

At university Ben discovered a talent for petty larceny. Endowed with the grace of a hunting cat, perhaps a legacy from his desert ancestors, he could climb any wall and slide across any roof top without being detected. The thefts were almost always discovered, eventually. The thief never apprehended. No one linked the skinny little Arab with the crimes.

Ben was short, quiet, and shy. He kept his jet black, frizzy hair neat and tidy. He dressed well, without ostentation. His only obvious vanity was a thin pencil line of moustache. Examining it in the mirror each day, he was convinced it made him look more mature. Ben worked hard at his studies and kept out of trouble. He had few friends. He was considered to be a loner and he was often rather lonely. Yet, basically, he was quite happy.

In three years, until a month before he graduated in the top ten percent for that year, Ben managed to purloin well over ten thousand dollars in cash and valuables. He didn't need the money. His proud father took care of all his expenses. Ben simply found intellectual stimulation in outwitting his victims, as well as the police. He was proud of his success in both his chosen fields of endeavour, academic and semi-professional. Undecided about his immediate future, Ben searched for ways to combine all his skills for one purpose. Politics, he admitted to himself with a smile, would require all his talents.

April Young was about to lose her seventh job since high school when she met Ben at the party. Indifferent to education and its values, April had drifted uselessly through school. Once in the work force she continued to show little inclination to achieve anything, other than her weekly pay. A factory worker father with a passion for beer, football, baseball, and nothing else, and a mother more interested in gossip than her children, clouded her youth. Beaten by her father for the slightest misdemeanor and ignored by her mother, April saw little or no future for herself. Unless a drastic change presented itself, her lot would be that of her mother and her neighbours; a barely sustainable marriage, unwanted pregnancies, little money, and never-ending housework. A life of drudgery. April didn't know how to achieve it, but she knew, for certain, she wanted more. Much more.

April lost her virginity at fourteen to a tough talking nineteen-year-old. She didn't enjoy the experience, though she did learn from it. Once she realized she was 'sitting on a gold mine,' as her older brother regularly informed her, April made use of her natural investment. At fifteen, to earn extra money, she began distributing her favours among her father's co-workers from the furniture factory on the outskirts of Buffalo. The back seats of cars, parked in the gloom of darkened alleys, became her place of business. She grew up bitter and hard. At the age of twenty-two she knew she either had to get out or accept her futureless fate.

Taken to the crowded party in Buffalo, where few people seemed to know each other, she was abandoned by her escort minutes after they arrived. At the Saturday night bash, where there were more illegal substances than alcohol, April watched the dusky-skinned Ben systematically robbing many of the other guests. She was fascinated. Not only could he remove a wallet from a back pocket without attracting the stoned owner's attention, he could rifle it and then return it, still without getting caught. April quickly realized that this boy, he didn't look old enough to be called a man in spite of his moustache, robbed as much for fun as for profit. She saw her opportunity and she took it.

Ben's basement apartment in Syracuse wasn't really big enough for two. A bookcase, every shelf lined with volumes in English, French, and Arabic, took up much of one wall. More books and magazines were stacked on the floor. A couch and an easy chair, both straying onto a deep pile Berber carpet, almost filled the rest of the living room space. Tucked in the corner, a small television looked out of place. The kitchen and dining area were cramped. A cheap unpainted wooden table, covered with newspapers, and two odd chairs were the only furniture. A three-quarter size bed, neatly made, and an old wardrobe made up the bedroom complement. The bathroom was clean though the sink had a thin crack in it. The shower curtain, a multi coloured plastic one, needed replacing. April moved in the night of the party anyway.

Long before she was twenty April had discovered the art of keeping a man in place. "Fuck him regularly and he'll do anything you want," she told her few friends. In contrast, Ben's experience of the opposite sex was non-existent until April entered his life. That first night, long before the cold dawn broke and tried to lure him to his senses, April took Ben through a whirlwind of fantasies and taught him how much he needed her. By the time it finally got light Ben was asleep with a smile on his face, exhausted after a marathon whirl of sexual excess. April lay on her back, unmoving beside him, her hands clasped together under the covers, a cautious gleam – close to triumph – in her eyes. When Ben awoke, just before eleven that morning, April was still there. Without a word she started on him again. As the day turned once again to night April knew, for certain, Ben would never be able to leave her.

Over the next week she re-organized the apartment until it was, at least, comfortable enough for two. She persuaded Ben to dump the piles of newspapers and magazines.

"There's no room here for that crap. It makes the place look real untidy. And we need a new shower curtain. Gimme some money, I'll go shopping."

Having left home with only the clothes she stood up in, April desperately needed to go back to Buffalo to collect her limited, but carefully acquired wardrobe. Picking a time when she was sure her father would be at work and her mother out shopping, she persuaded Ben to drive her home to collect all her possessions. Ben stayed in the car while April hurriedly filled two suitcases. Seeing a ten-dollar bill and some loose change on the coffee table in front of the television, she pocketed the lot and left the house. April never went back again.

By day Ben attended lectures or studied. The teaching jobs he had described to his parents were figments of his imagination, nothing more. April, at Ben's urging, got a job packing groceries part time in a supermarket. At night the unlikely accomplices traded skills. Ben tried to teach April the basics of his illicit craft. Unfortunately, she had not been blessed with his natural grace. Compared to Ben, she was a clumsy pickpocket, sure to get caught if allowed to work without the strictest of supervision. April, in her turn, taught Ben delights he had only dreamed of alone in the darkness. Inept at most things, due to a lack of education and interest, April was a naturally talented whore in bed. Her teenage years had simply improved a latent ability. Ben couldn't believe there were so many uses for a mouth.

"Hey, Ben," April whined a week after Ben's graduation, "why don't we go after some real money for a change? Let's rob a bank or somethin', huh?"

Ben shook his head distractedly without looking up from his magazine. April fumed. "Whaddya reading now?" Leaving the sink, she dried her hands and tore the magazine from him.

"Diamonds! Fuckin' diamonds. Boy, wouldn't I like to wear that round my neck?" April showed Ben the photograph. He glanced at it, touched the page with his finger tip; looked up at April. Her eyes, for the first time since they met, were shining. "We could rob jewellery shops," she said, meaning it.

Ben took the magazine back, studied it purposefully for a few minutes, saying nothing. April folded her thin white arms across her chest, waiting. "Well, whaddya think?"

"Yeah," Ben nodded to himself, answering mechanically, his brain working overtime. "Yeah, we could. We'll have to be careful. But we could do it. Let me think about it for a while."

Ben spent long days researching bank robberies and jewellery store heists in the library. At night he studied city and state maps. Ever impatient, April nagged at him daily.

"How much longer we gonna wait? I'm bored, Ben."

"When I'm ready, we'll do it. Not until then. Wait. Just wait. I'll tell you when. Now, go watch television or something."

After careful consideration Ben decided he and April would hit a jewellery store, but not locally. Instead they would cross the Canadian border in Niagara Falls. Canada seemed like a safer place to try a real robbery than New York State. The experiment was almost their last.

April walked into the shop wearing a new two-piece navy blue suit, high heel shoes, and a large unmarked imitation leather shoulder bag, all courtesy of Ben. The smile, happy at last, was all her own. He followed, also smart, wearing a grey pin-stripe suit. To a casual observer he looked like a young accountant or a banker on his way up,

"Good morning," the owner greeted them affably, anticipating a lucrative sale.

"Morning," Ben answered then, without further pleasantry, "Now move back against the wall."

Ben's hand, with two fingers stuck out to simulate a gun, pointed at the owner through his jacket pocket. "I said, move. Now sit on the floor. Hands on your head."

April scooped two trays of rings and an assortment of gold necklaces from the counter top. While she worked, the shopkeeper glared from one to the other as Ben stood guard.

"Okay, you ready?" he asked April. She nodded. "Keep watch for a minute."

Quickly Ben tied the shopkeeper's hands behind him and wrapped a pocket handkerchief round his mouth.

"Right, you go first."

April sauntered out the front door, calling out a cheerful, "Thank you," as she turned the sign to 'closed.' Ben left by the back entrance, walking briskly to where the Mustang was parked on a side street a block away. He stripped off his suit jacket, pulled on a blue windbreaker, baseball cap and dark glasses. April strolled in the opposite direction, turned left then right. When she saw Ben's car approaching minutes later, she waited on the side of the road to be picked up.

No more than fifty paces from her a little boy ran into the road after a balloon, directly in the path of Ben's Mustang. Ben had no choice. He hit the brakes hard and skidded to the left, catching the child a slight, glancing blow with the right fender. April watched in horror from a distance as the mini drama unfolded, trying to assess her next move.

A handful of people rushed to the scene: April faded into the background. As soon as he could, if he could, Ben would pick her up at their planned emergency location, outside the city hall. She was to wait there for one hour, if possible, then, if Ben had not shown up, she was to make her own way home.

Ben got out of the car shaking, his nerves agitated as a leaf in a storm. Tenderly he held the crying child, feeling him for broken bones. The boy was scared but otherwise unhurt, as far as Ben could tell. A woman in her late twenties grabbed the boy from Ben's arms as a police patrol car pulled up behind the Mustang.

"Jimmy, Jimmy, are you alright, darling?" she hugged the boy to her.

Ben stood in confusion, helpless as one policeman told him to stay put while the other radioed for an ambulance.

"License please, sir," the policeman held out his hand as Ben fumbled in his wallet, "and car registration too."

Ben reached into the glove compartment and pulled out the blue plastic holder containing insurance, registration, and automobile club membership. He handed everything to the policeman, pleased to see his hands hardly shook at all.

Witnesses, including an approaching traffic warden, insisted the driver was not at fault. An hour after the incident Ben was allowed to leave without further hindrance. He detoured round a couple of city blocks and cruised towards City Hall. April was still waiting; praying Ben would come for her. She still held the proceeds of the robbery in her bag.

In the jewellers the unlucky shopkeeper had finally managed to free himself. Hurriedly he dialed the police. "I told you we should have bought that surveillance camera," he complained to his still-bound wife as he listened to the ringing, "but no, you didn't wanna do that 'cause the salesman was such a smooth talker. Hello, police? Yeah I've been robbed."

Taking care not to exceed the speed limit, Ben and April turned onto the bridge over the Niagara Gorge. Off to their right

72

clouds of spray and mist from the thundering Horseshoe Falls hung in wet veils over the crowds of sightseers lining the footpaths. Deep in the gorge the *Maid of the Mist* carried her excited passengers into the gaping, soaking maw at the foot of the horseshoe. The miniature figures, clad in black oilskins, were just visible against the white water. Closer, the jagged edges of the American Falls glistened under the weight of its own turbulent cascade tumbling to the river far below.

Halfway across the bridge, where the flags of two friendly nations fluttered side by side, Ben and April crossed back into the States. Safe in America again, they both let out a huge sigh of relief.

"Shit, man, that was close," April shouted.

"Keep it down, we're not home yet," Ben warned as they slowed at the US Customs barrier. The official, noting the New York registration plate, leaned down to the window as they stopped and asked, "Both US citizens? Where do you live?"

"Yes. Syracuse."

"How long have you been in Canada?"

"About three hours," Ben answered truthfully. "We just went to see the falls from the Canadian side." Not the whole truth but enough to satisfy officialdom.

"Did you make any purchases?"

Once again Ben answered truthfully, "No, sir, not a thing. We've just been sightseeing."

The officer waved them through with a cheerful, "Have a nice day," following them.

"I think we'll stay on this side of the border from now on," Ben told April as the customs post dwindled in the distance, "It's a lot safer".

For a few weeks they robbed small jewellery stores in five neighbouring states and sold the goods to a Lebanese fence in Yonkers. They were discreet, careful, and no one ever got hurt. Never again after that first scare in Canada, did they enter a store together. The pair alternated the jobs, one going into the store, the other staying in the car. They never wore the same clothes on two jobs. They never looked the same. Always April disguised the one to take the risk. Crime, she discovered, suited her. She was beginning to show a previously hidden store of resourcefulness.

Ben soon realized that, though most small jewellery stores had a miniature camera tucked between the ceiling and the wall, rarely did anyone watch the video recording until well after an incident. Even those cameras linked to police stations or security companies were rarely watched constantly. The chances of being spotted during a robbery were, he calculated, small enough to make it worthwhile. April's simple disguises, and the speed with which she worked, made it difficult to make a positive identification of the perpetrator anyway.

Never, after their first robbery, did they use the same car. Ben became skilled at auto theft, keeping each car no longer than necessary for any one job. Often he changed cars two or three times in one day to cover his trail. The pair always wore gloves. The cars were always abandoned clean and undamaged.

Police in five states held open files on jewellery store robberies. Confusing eye witness descriptions listed a variety of suspects. No names were mentioned.

* * *

Tango Perez sat in a wicker chair on his veranda. His eyes were closed, his chin rested on his chest. A dribble of saliva ran from his moist open lips. It trickled through two days growth of grey stubble down to his stained, white silk shirt. He was asleep. In one hand, balanced precariously on his ample paunch, the remains of a glass of rum slopped in time with his heavy breathing. On the mahogany floor at his feet an empty bottle pointed forlornly at the distant volcanic cone of Mount Irazu.

A light breeze, roaming at random across the range from the snow-clad slopes, cooled the late afternoon sun. It reached up, gusting in whispers, to play with a silvery lock of Tango's hair; all that remained of his former beauty. The once handsome face contorted as excess wind in its bloated body escaped in a raucous fart. The sound, reminiscent of a trombone being played badly, echoed across the veranda. A hummingbird, hovering with its beak probing the nucleus of a crimson bougainvillea climbing the trellis at one end, flew away in alarm. Tango snorted and belched, opening his hand. The rum spilled down his belly and mingled with his urine-stained cream trousers. The glass rolled to the floor. It bounced once, without breaking, and rotated to a stop, facing the open neck of the bottle as if demanding another drink.

Stirring a little, Tango changed position releasing another humid fart as he did so. His manservant, Carlos, came slowly on to the veranda, wrinkling his nose in disgust at the smell and the sight of his life-long employer.

"Senor Perez, wake up, Senor Perez," he shook Tango's heavy shoulder hard. "Come on, you drunken old bastard, let's get you cleaned up."

Groaning under the dead weight of a man nearly twice his size and the same age, Carlos pulled Tango from the chair. He wound one arm round his waist and draped Tango's left arm over his own thin shoulders. Bent almost double, he half carried half dragged the comatose figure to the bathroom. Without ceremony Carlos dropped his burden on the white tiled floor. He stripped off each item of Tango's clothing and threw them into a laundry basket. The hand-tooled riding boots he placed outside the door to be cleaned later. Tango snored through it all.

With a sigh of resignation, Carlos filled a bucket with warm soapy water and knelt slowly at Tango's side. Getting down on one's knees at sixty-seven was not easy. Getting up again was even harder. Gently, as if bathing his own son, Carlos washed the bloated body all over. Using a straight razor, he shaved away the stubble until Tango's chin shone as if just polished. Satisfied with his work, Carlos rose stiffly to his feet holding tightly to the towel rail for support.

"Now, Senor," he grunted, "it is time to wake up."

Tango lay flat on his back still snoring peacefully, his legs apart and his arms outstretched. Carlos turned on a cold tap and let it run for a few minutes. Nodding to himself with a gleam of amusement in his old eyes, he turned the tap on full and switched the dial to shower. Holding the flexible hose in one hand and the shower head in the other, he tested the temperature before positioning himself upright between his victim's feet. From there he aimed the icy jets at Tango's groin. The expected reaction was delayed by a few seconds. As his genitals shriveled at the cold blast, Tango woke up suddenly, roaring like an injured bull as he tried to sit. Carlos re-directed his aim, catching him full in the face. Tango fell back, his head hitting the floor hard.

"Good evening, Senor," Carlos greeted him cordially. "Do you feel better now?"

"You little weasel, Carlos, I'll skin you alive," Tango bellowed following his threat with a stream of profanities as he rubbed the back of his head.

Carlos turned off the tap and replaced the shower head. "You'd better get dressed, Senor. You have an important visitor coming before dinner."

Tango blinked and shook his head. "Who?"

"Senor Fuentes, the bank manager. He is coming to talk to you about money, I think," Carlos replied.

"Oh shit, what time is it?"

"It's five-thirty. He's coming at seven. You must be ready, Senor."

"Is that fat crook coming for dinner?" Tango groaned. "He eats enough for three men."

"No, Senor, he is only coming for one drink and to talk to you."

Fuentes arrived late. Tango was already halfway through his second rum of the evening when the banker's black Mercedes drew up outside. Carlos ushered the guest into the library where Tango waited.

"Senor Fuentes," he stood up, his face beaming, as he extended his hand in welcome. "Please come in. Such a pleasure to see you again. Will you join me in a drink?"

"Good evening, Senor Perez. Thank you, I'll have a small glass of white wine."

The banker was a busy man, and he had little time to spare for the indulgences of people like Tango Perez. As soon as he was seated with a drink in his hand he got straight to the point.

"Your account is heavily overdrawn again, Senor Perez. Something must be done about it immediately." He looked sternly at his host, "You can't go on living like this, on other people's money. If you can't come up with enough to clear your overdraft by the end of the month, I will have to adopt serious measures."

"By the end of the month," Tango moaned, "that's only one week away. How much do you need?"

Fuentes told him and watched as Tango turned as white as his shirt. "I had no idea it was so much," he grunted, looking down at his drink as he spoke.

The banker stood up. "Until the end of the month, Senor. No longer." Then he was gone, leaving his drink hardly touched.

Tango sat perfectly still for a few moments, his mind turning over the implications of the banker's warning. He couldn't sell the ranch. It was already mortgaged beyond his capability to pay. The cattle which grazed on his land were no longer his. The plantations had long been sold off. His polo ponies, once a useful source of income, were in the distant past. There was only one thing for it. Only one way he could get out of the financial hole he had dug so energetically for himself for so many years. His only choice was to sell his sole remaining treasure; the *Namib Star*. Even that, he reminded himself ruefully, was locked up in the banker's vaults.

"Carlos," he bellowed in frustration, "get me another fucking drink."

* * *

April held her right hand in her pocket. It looked menacing under the dark blue cloth. With her left she threw a bag at the jeweller in Salem, Massachusetts.

"Fill it with those rings and those necklaces," she pointed at the trays she wanted.

The man looked down at something behind the display case and bent towards it. April guessed his intention and threw a tight-fisted punch, catching him on the bridge of his nose. With eyes watering from the blow and nose bleeding into his hands, the jeweller was disorientated for the three seconds it took April to reach his side of the counter. She grabbed the shotgun from under the displays and rammed the barrels into his stomach.

"Don't move or I'll blow you in half," she snarled, vaguely aware that she had never held a gun of any kind in her life.

"Now fill the bag like you were told. And those. And those." She pointed to the items she wanted as the jeweller scooped up trays of rings and costume jewellery, stuffing them in April's bag. Her heart pounding with a mix of excitement and fear, she backed out of the store and strode quickly along the sidewalk to Ben's waiting car.

"Go, Sugar," she ordered before the door closed, "I got us some great stuff, and I got a gun."

April held the twin barrels across her lap and patted them affectionately. "With this baby we can really hit the big time."

Ben glanced at the shotgun in horror. "What the fuck did you steal that for? We don't need a gun; I keep telling you that."

"Well we've got one now, so quit fucking complaining."

"That wasn't smart, April. If that gun's registered we're in the shit," Ben moaned, never taking his eyes off the road. "With that thing you're taking us into a completely different realm. Before it was just robbery. Now it's robbery with violence, or something like that. A whole new equation."

"Don't worry about it. With this we don't need violence; or your fuckin' equations."

The owner reported the theft of the gun at the same time as he reported the hold up. The police booked him for not having a firearm permit.

"It's just not been your day, sir, has it," the young constable told him with a hint of a smirk on his otherwise straight face.

April persuaded Ben in bed that afternoon that the shotgun was protection for them and a deterrent against retaliation by shopkeepers. Convinced she meant it, Ben agreed – as long as they used it as a threat, nothing more. April accepted his decision.

"I'll keep it loaded, just in case," she told him, "but I'll always have the safety catch on."

April enjoyed the feel of the gun in her hands. It made her feel strong, powerful, indestructible. Any time she felt nervous or unsure of herself, she held the gun in her arms like a doll. It was comforting. She really liked that shotgun. One day, she promised herself, she would pull those triggers and blast the guts out of some unsuspecting jeweller. Just one wrong move, that's all she wanted. One wrong move. She said nothing to Ben of her thoughts. He was the mastermind. April was content to take the risks.

On the eve of their next job April sat in front of the television cleaning the already immaculate shotgun with a rag. She took her time, polishing the barrels lovingly.

"Why do you keep doing that?" Ben asked. "It's always clean because it's never used".

April said nothing. She simply shook her head and went on with her cleaning, lost in her own thoughts. There was no sex the night before the robbery; there never was. April was too tense for any intimacy. Ben went over the plans for a final time while she listened carefully. When Ben went to bed, rarely nervous, April sat alone in the darkness for long hours, with the shotgun beside her, thinking about the coming day. Eventually she fell asleep cradling the shotgun, dreaming of pulling those delicate triggers.

* * *

For once Tango was sober. Wearing a suit and a clean shirt and tie, carefully maintained by Carlos, he sat in Senor Fuentes's office, listening carefully.

"Antonio, my old friend," the bank manager spoke soothingly, reassuring him, "it is the only way. You must agree to sell the diamond. I have contacted certain people in Europe on your behalf. Sotheby's in Geneva would be delighted to hold an auction. Such a beautiful stone will attract the very best buyers to their city."

"How much?" Tango asked grumpily.

"How much what? How much will you earn? Is that your question?"

Tango nodded unhappily, "Si, how much money will I get?"

"I'm told you can expect about ten million pounds sterling. Out of that you should pay their commission. Then you have to pay all your debts, Senor, and they are many."

"How much?" Tango asked again. "How much will be left?"

"Two, maybe three million pounds, enough for you to live comfortably, and quietly, for the rest of your life. You are too old to be a playboy any longer anyway."

"When will this auction take place?"

"As soon as possible. I just have to make one phone call, that is all."

Tango thought for a moment, his mind playing with an idea. The remnants of a once active business brain ticked relentlessly through a concept.

"Okay, I agree," he stood up, facing Fuentes squarely, "but first, I want my diamond put on display in Antwerp where it was first cut. Perhaps for a week, no more. That will build interest and hold the price up, plus we can make some money on the exhibition. I will organize that myself."

Fuentes considered the idea for a moment. Secretly he was pleased to see Tango taking a positive role in the venture.

"It is a good suggestion," he agreed. "Perhaps you should go to Antwerp with one of my insurance people to make the necessary arrangements. Meanwhile I will talk to Sotheby's and set a date. Also, I will contact a bank colleague in Antwerp for safe storage of the diamond until the exhibition."

Tango left San Jose a month later on a commercial flight to Madrid, with a connection to Brussels. A taciturn young insurance specialist travelled with him. From Brussels they took a train to Antwerp. Unknown to Tango, the diamond crossed the Atlantic at roughly the same time as his flight, though by a more northerly route. Fuentes, taking only a slight gamble on the high insurance value, sent an innocent looking parcel by DHL courier. The diamond was in the vaults of the Generale Banque in Antwerp before Tango and his aide arrived at their hotel.

82

Chapter 6

April waited patiently for the jewellery store in the small New Hampshire town to open. They were three minutes late by her watch. Inside a handsome young man put on his suit jacket as he glanced at the row of clocks on the wall. He checked his own wristwatch. Right on time. Through the glass door he could see a well-dressed woman with flame red hair waiting for him to open.

"Coming," he called brightly, stepping to the door. He slid back three dead bolts and opened the door. "Good morn..." his voice tailed off as he was confronted with the business end of a gleaming double-barreled shotgun.

"What the Hell? Forget it, lady." He tried to close the door on the deadly barrels. He was a fraction too late. April already had her feet braced firmly against it. Holding the shotgun diagonally across her chest she pushed him roughly inside and back against a counter. She aimed the gun at his waist and held up her bag.

"Fill it, you bastard, now," she snarled. Praying the gun wasn't loaded, the brave, foolhardy, young man made a grab for the barrels. April immediately pulled both triggers sharply. Nothing happened. She pulled the triggers again without success. As the plucky jeweller fought her for possession of the gun she suddenly broke free. Swinging the shotgun in a vicious underhand arc she brought the stock up between his legs as hard as she could. The jeweller screamed in pain and doubled over on the floor. April kicked him in the head, smashed a display case with the gun and looted the contents. Sliding the weapon into a special long inside pocket on her coat she left the store, giving the recumbent jeweller another kick as she passed. Ben waited across the street.

In the car she told Ben, "The bastard tried to attack me. I pulled the triggers but the fucking gun doesn't work. I had to hit him with it."

Ben was appalled at the coldness in April's voice and furious that she had broken her word.

"You promised no violence," Ben raged as he drove off. "What the hell is the matter with you? No fucking violence. Understand?"

"Fuck you, it's not your life," April spat back. "I'm the one taking the risks." She felt the shotgun nestling against her and ran her hand along its length. Suddenly she started to laugh.

Ben looked at her sideways. "What's so funny?"

"I left the fucking safety catches on, no wonder it didn't work." She laughed again.

Ben shook his head disbelievingly, "Jeez, I'm glad you did. Leave them on. If that gun had gone off you would have cut him in two."

They ditched the first of Ben's stolen cars, a Chevrolet with Pennsylvania license plates, in a parking lot and took the second to Albany. There on a quiet tree-lined boulevard they transferred to the Mustang and went straight to Yonkers. Ben hated to keep stolen property near them any longer than necessary. He adamantly refused to ever take the goods home. Once free of the incriminating evidence, the pair returned immediately to the apartment in Syracuse. Ben felt the long detours to get rid of stolen cars a necessary part of their style.

Once safely home April grilled a couple of burgers while Ben had his customary after robbery shower. He had found a strong

84

wish to cleanse himself as soon as possible after the event. April's immediate needs were quite different.

Once they had eaten and the dishes washed and put away by Ben, April stood up and peeled off her red blouse. With her eyes locked on Ben's she slowly reached behind her and unhooked her black bra. Ben was mesmerized. No matter how many times she did it, always after every robbery, he was transfixed. April slid the flimsy garment off her white shoulders and let it fall to the floor. Her smooth rounded breasts, a little small though beautifully formed, thrust out temptingly. She flicked a finger over each pink nipple, watching Ben lick his lips as the tantalizing twins stood to attention.

Ben leaned back against his chair, his legs stuck out straight. He kept his eyes on April's. She dropped her eyes to his groin, seeing with satisfaction that he already had an erection. April unzipped her tight black skirt, pulled it down over her hips and stepped out of it. Ben got up, his eyes wide, as April slowly gyrated out of her pantyhose. She hooked her fingers in the waist band of her tiny black panties and slid them down her thighs. Ben took a step forward, undoing his belt at the same time.

"Come here, Sugar," April crooned. "Come and see what I've got for you." She reached into Ben's pants as he cupped her breasts in his hands. "Now Baby," April breathed at him, "Now!"

The ritual never varied. April teased, Ben watched. April gave the orders on these occasions; Ben was happy to obey.

The New York State Police had three dossiers on the unknown jewel thieves. One, a gift from their Ontario Provincial Police counterparts across the border, described a couple in their early twenties. She, white, with light brown eyes and long blonde curls was tall, perhaps five feet eight or nine. He was dark skinned, dark eyes, with black hair and a moustache and a few inches shorter. This file noted the clothes they had worn to rob the jewellers in Niagara Falls. It had not been cross-referenced or associated in any way with the file on the boy who had escaped injury in the road accident.

The second file was on a tall red-headed woman in her early thirties. It noted that she was armed with a sawn-off shotgun and was dangerous. No mention was made of an accomplice. A third file offered a perfect description of April as she was dressed in the Canadian robbery, only she was described as being short, possibly no more than five feet two. April liked to change her shoe styles as often as she changed her wigs and her clothes. The police assumed she had worked with an accomplice, probably a getaway driver. They had no description of car or driver.

The police files did not, in fact, include a make, colour or registration of any of the getaway cars, if there were any. They did contain lists of cars stolen within reasonable driving distance from the scene of the robbery, that day and the day before. Those which had been found quickly, usually within a day in multi-level car parks or on quiet residential streets, were highlighted. It did little good, but it did show a pattern, of sorts. Ben was highly unlikely to steal the same car twice. Never did he steal a Mustang, or any car which vaguely resembled it. No Mustangs were listed as being stolen and later left unharmed. The police were frustrated, but patient. One day, they knew, their quarry would make a mistake.

As the police scratched their heads in confusion over the identities and whereabouts of the jewellery thieves, April abruptly changed her style. On the morning of a planned trip to Lebanon, Pennsylvania, in the heart of the Deutsch farming communities, April dressed in particular care. She put aside the high heel boots and flat heeled shoes. Pulling on a skin-tight body stocking, April made sure her breasts were flattened. Instead of a skirt, April pulled on a pair of faded blue denims over her bare legs. She put grey wool socks on her feet and laced a pair of grubby running shoes over them. A baggy, blue-checked shirt, one of Ben's, replaced the normal blouse. Over the complete ensemble she wore a black leather jacket. Tucking her short hair under a woollen skull cap, she examined herself in the mirror. As intended, she looked like a fresh-faced teenage boy. With a nod of approval at her reflection, she picked up a bag with a change of clothes, the shotgun, and a leather pouch.

"Okay, I'm ready, Ben."

"Hey, that's good. You look like a guy."

"That's the idea, stupid."

Ben ignored the insult. "Come on, let's go. We've got a long drive ahead of us."

With Ben at the wheel they took the most direct route to Williamsport. From there he followed the west bank of the meandering Susquehanna River south towards Harrisburg. In the heart of the lovely Pennsylvania countryside April saw something which made her spin round in her seat.

"Did you see those guys? They goin' to a party or somethin'?" April looked back down the road at the two strangely dressed men. "Did you see them, Ben?"

"Yeah, I saw them. They're Amish people, I think."

"Amish? What's that? Ain't they American?"

"Course they are. Used to be German, I think. Some religious sect, Mennonites, or something. Farmers mostly."

"Why'd they dress like that and ride a horse and cart?"

"It's part of their religion, I guess."

"Why don't they drive a car like everyone else?"

"Like I told you, it's something to do with their religion."

"No shit. You wouldn't catch me dressed like that," April continued to look back in amazement. "Shit man, that's real weird, you know?"

In Harrisburg Ben relinquished the steering wheel to April. "I'll meet you in Reading, in the airport parking lot," he reminded her as he got out.

True to his word, less than half an hour after April parked the Mustang, Ben sauntered towards her. "I've left the new car on the other side. Let's go."

Without haste the two ambled to Ben's latest acquisition. Showing no sign of nervousness, nothing to make any other drivers uneasy or suspicious, they chatted and laughed like any other teenage boys as they opened the doors. Once on the road again they became serious.

"You're going in the back door this time," Ben ran over the plan again as he drove the recently stolen Buick towards

Lebanon, "and you'll leave the same way. I'll be right outside in the lane."

As they passed the front of their targeted jeweller April glanced through the window. "No customers in there that I can see," she advised.

Ben turned right and right again into the paved lane. "Go for it; and be careful," he warned.

The engine ticked over quietly as Ben watched through the windshield and all his mirrors at once. Not a soul in sight. April had only been in the store for thirty seconds or so when the shattering blast of a shotgun split the air. "Oh, Allah, no!" Cried Ben. April came running out waving the gun in one hand and the pouch in the other. "Go! Go! Go!" she yelled as she jumped into the already moving vehicle.

Ben took a corner on two wheels and raced down another lane. He screeched to a halt at the end and looked left and right. A middle-aged man walking his dog waited at the curb. The man glanced at the two in the car, shaking his head in disgust at their haste. Nearby a couple of parked cars were empty. There was no other traffic. Desperately trying to control his nerves Ben forced himself to drive sedately away from the scene.

"We need a parking lot, quickly," he ordered. "We have to ditch this car."

April scanned the map of the immediate area. "Turn left, go two blocks then right, there's one there." Ben kept control, made the required turns, and parked the car. "Wait here," he growled at her. Less than a minute later a white Cadillac pulled up behind the Buick. April got in and Ben wheeled the big car away from town. Neither of them spoke a word until they had dumped the Caddy in Reading and were safely on their way to Yonkers in the Mustang.

Keeping uncharacteristically silent, April studied Ben closely. She could see he was ready to explode. "Are you mad at me, Sugar?" she asked unnecessarily.

"What happened back there? Tell me. Now! What the fuck happened?" Ben screamed at April. "I told you many times, no fucking violence. Did you shoot someone?" he finished in almost a whisper.

"Yeah, the creep pulled a fuckin' gun on me. I had no choice. Got him right in the balls, too," April replied with obvious satisfaction.

"Is he dead? Did you kill him?" Ben, almost in tears, turned ashen at the thought.

"How the fuck should I know. Would you still be alive if you got your balls shot off?"

Ben pounded the steering wheel with one gloved hand. "You stupid bitch. You stupid fucking bitch. Now we're really in the shit."

April ignored the outburst. As Ben drove, his eyes narrowed and focused on the road ahead, she took off the blue shirt and woollen hat. Removing a couple of pins, she peeled off a short black wig to reveal her own mousy hair. Unfolding a dark brown sweater from her bag she pulled it on over her head. April held up her bag.

"We didn't get much this time, only a handful of gold chains and a few diamond rings. I hope they're real."

Ben ignored her, his eyes stayed wrinkled, staring down the highway into the distance. April settled back against the seat and closed her eyes. Ben, she was sure, would come around eventually. Until then he was best left to himself. For half an hour she kept still, the shotgun beside her, thinking how good it had felt to pull those triggers. She looked sideways at Ben and felt a familiar stirring inside. "Pull, over, Sugar," she said, touching his face. "I need you real bad right now."

Ben roughly swatted her hand away, wiping his mouth with the back of his hand. "Don't fuck about, April."

"Don't fuck about, April," she mimicked, shaking her head from side to side. She leaned towards him and put one hand on his thigh. Slowly, she moved up to his groin. He pushed her hand away.

"Fuck off, April. I'm not in the mood."

As he pulled off the highway outside Yonkers April sat up straight. "Now we're safe again. No descriptions of me. There's nothing to worry about, Sugar," she prodded Ben in the ribs with a sharp forefinger. "Let's get rid of this junk fast and get home, I need a good fuck."

The night smelled of wet, falling leaves when they at last parked the Mustang in their reserved stall outside the apartment block. Rain slanted down, aided by a rising wind. They were both soaked before they reached the building. April was as good as her word this time. Instead of drying off she went into her striptease as soon as the door closed behind them. It wasn't long before her pale, slender, almost hairless body was locked with Ben's. She gripped him tightly around his waist, holding his chest of black curly hair against her bare breasts, as he thrust roughly into her on the floor. "Oh yeah, oh yeah. That's what I needed," April moaned in his ear.

Television news that evening reported an armed robbery at a jeweller's in Lebanon, Pennsylvania. A sixty-three-year-old man had been shot in the lower abdomen. He died a few hours later in hospital. The police were looking for two young men, one wearing blue jeans, a blue check shirt and a black leather jacket. There was no description of the other man, only that he was wearing a black balaclava. They were said to be armed and dangerous. The report added that they were believed to be driving a white 1985 Cadillac stolen from a parking lot in Lebanon after they had dumped their getaway Buick. A later news bulletin advised that the Cadillac had been found in the parking lot at Reading Airport. It was being checked for fingerprints while the police went through all airline passenger records for flights into and out of Reading that day.

April listened with growing amusement. Ben took note of everything that was said too. He was far more concerned than April. He knew the police were not fools. Sooner or later there would be a knock on the door.

"We'd better lay low for a few weeks and make some different plans," he said. "We have to let this cool down. When you start using guns the cops get really pissed. They are looking for two murderers now. You and me."

"We're just like Bonnie and Clyde," April laughed at him. "I seen it in the movies. They were just like us, except that Clyde had a gun and you don't and you know how to be a lover and Clyde didn't."

"I'm nothing like Clyde Barrow. He was stupid and dangerous. He got shot. I won't."

"Well I'm like Bonnie, I reckon. She wasn't stupid. She even wrote poetry. Listen"

April stood in the middle of the room and recited,

"They call them cold-blooded killers;
They say they are heartless and mean;
But I say this with pride,
That I once knew Clyde
When he was honest and upright and clean."

"Clyde Barrow was still stupid. So was Bonnie Parker," Ben interrupted before April could get into more verses.

"Bonnie Parker was not stupid," April shouted. "She was real smart."

Ben had the last words as he turned away. "She got shot, didn't she?"

They waited throughout the night, Ben worrying about an unwanted knock on the door. For three days he worried but there was no sudden visit from the police. Down in Pennsylvania the robbery was being treated as a copycat version of all the holdups in New York and the New England States. A copy which this time had resulted in murder. They were not looking for a woman. April was convinced they had nothing to worry about.

"They're not looking for us," she insisted, "because they don't know who we are. Let's go back to work, I'm bored."

Finally, after a month had passed without any sign of suspicion from the New York State, or any other police force, Ben admitted they might try one more job. "Then we're moving," he warned April, "We're gonna get out of this country."

"Hey, that's great, man," April shouted with excitement. "Where we goin'? When?"

"Soon enough. We'll get you a passport, then we're going to France, to Paris. I know people there. First, we have another job to do. Now listen," Ben ordered April, "don't use the gun. It's a prop, nothing more. If you use it again I swear to almighty Allah I'll hand you over to the cops myself."

April's retort was predictably crude.

* * *

Inspector Etienne Delvaux was in a foul mood. His day was not going well at all and it wasn't even light outside yet. He lit another Belga, sucking the smoke in until it reached the very corners of his lungs. He exhaled slowly, the evil smelling fumes billowing and swirling in a pale blue haze through the office's dull light. Coal black eyes narrowed as he waited. Impatiently he tossed a telephone directory to the floor behind him and scooped three plastic coffee cups into the garbage to his left.

The detective inspector was responsible to his superiors for policing crime in Antwerp's diamond district. Any problem in that area, at any time, meant he got involved. At a few minutes after four o'clock that morning he had been called from his bed. A body had been found in an alley close to the Diamond Museum on Lange Herentalsstraat. One look at the corpse told him all he wanted to know. The dead man was a wino, well known to many of Delvaux's officers. He looked and smelled as though he had drunk himself to death. An autopsy would verify his conclusion.

"Get him out of here," Delvaux ordered. Turning to the cop who had phoned him, he stabbed a thick finger into the middle of his chest, "You didn't need to call me to look at a dead drunk. Next time – think."

Wide awake, Delvaux went to his office. There was no fresh coffee available. Not known for his sympathetic nature at the best of times, the disgruntled detective roared at a subordinate to remedy the situation. He couldn't concentrate without coffee first thing in the morning. While he waited, Delvaux smoked and scanned the papers on his desk. He looked through them,

92

absorbing the words, seeing nothing. His mind was elsewhere.

He could have been tucked up in bed with his wife's buxom body curled up in his arms. He could be making love to her right now. A spasm in his groin and the beginnings of an erection made him groan softly. He shook the thought from his mind, grunting his thanks without looking up as a mug of strong black coffee was placed in front of him. Holding the mug in one huge black hand he leafed through the stack of papers again.

"What's this?" he read the note from the diamond museum advising him of a special exhibition planned for the following month. A single diamond, one of the most valuable in the world, was to spend a week in Antwerp on display before going to auction in Geneva. Delvaux grunted in annoyance, "Why can't they show it off in Amsterdam? I don't need more headaches."

94

Chapter 7   Europe

The idea of moving kept April in line to an extent. Another job guaranteed her acquiescence. She was tired of the cramped apartment, especially after the few weeks of enforced inactivity. She needed action and she needed it fast.

Atkinson Jewellers was to be their final heist in the USA. After Ben's decision to relocate, April was keen to travel. The idea of Paris exited her. The French capital suited Ben perfectly too. He had been brought up to speak fluent French and he could, he knew, disappear at will among the thousands of his fellow countrymen living in Paris if need be. Ben insisted April try to learn French.

"You have to," he pushed, "otherwise you won't know what the hell's going on."

He soon discovered April wasn't a great pupil. Her attention span was short and her patience for learning limited. She did, however, Ben admitted privately, make an effort on most days.

Their departure had been planned, by Ben, to the last detail. A few hours after the holdup they would be airborne for Paris.

April stepped out of the jewellery shop into the bright Connecticut sunshine, screwing up her eyes at the sudden light.

Lifting the sunglasses from the top of her head she adjusted them over her hazel eyes. Jauntily, without undue haste, she strode along the sidewalk. As she walked her blonde ringlets, falling comfortably to her shoulders, rustled like silk in the breeze. Dressed in a fashionable brown leather coat, which reached to the middle of her knees, and tan slacks, with a large matching leather bag over her shoulder, she was an average middle-class shopper in a reasonably affluent district. No one took any notice of her, except Ben, an olive-skinned young man in a dark blue Mercury outside a furniture store immediately opposite.

He started his engine as soon as April appeared, signalled left and pulled into the light Saturday afternoon traffic. At the first corner he turned right, cruised the length of the block, and took another right. At the stop sign he brought all four wheels to a standstill. Another car passed in front of him. With only one hand on the wheel he spun the power steering to follow. One block ahead, where the main street split the city, the traffic lights were red. Keeping a fraction below the speed limit he moved towards the lights. Only one car was waiting.

As he slowed, the brake lights on the Mercury glowed to match the traffic signals. The red beam went out and the green lit up. The car in front turned right without signaling.

"Jerk!" Ben grunted as he crossed the road. Clear of the intersection he slowed and stopped. April came out of the doorway of a book shop on the corner and got in as the car door swung open. In the distance the wail of a police siren sounded the first warning of trouble for someone.

"Let's go, Ben, but take it easy for chrissakes."

Ben didn't need to be told. As April ducked her head under the dashboard he coaxed the car up to thirty miles an hour and held it there. April sat up. The blonde ringlets were gone. In their place was a boyish head of short black hair.

Deftly she popped contact lenses from her eyes. The hazel disguise changed to steel grey reality.

A patrol car, siren still screaming, red and blue roof lights flashing, skidded to a halt outside Atkinson's Jewellers. With guns drawn two middle-aged policemen rushed in. Behind the counter a smartly dressed man in his mid-fifties was comforting a sobbing younger shop assistant. Seeing the sawn-off shotgun rammed between her father's legs had put the woman close to hysterics.

"You're too late, guys," Atkinson told the police reproachfully, "she's long gone by now."

Once out of the city, Ben drove with continued care. He bypassed New Haven and headed into Bridgeport. In a multi-story car park Ben drove to the fourth level. He parked the Mercury in a corner stall and the two walked unhurriedly down the stairs to the third level. When the Mercury was eventually recognized to have over-stayed its time, a police check would ascertain it had been stolen from a similar parking lot in New Haven the day of the robbery.

Ben and April stopped beside Ben's red Mustang. Ben took the shotgun and slid it quickly into a container under the front seat. April opened the trunk and tossed her leather coat on top of two bulging black carry-alls. She slammed the lid closed and got into the passenger's side. A black raincoat was folded on the seat behind her covering an empty backpack, the kind preferred by students to carry their school books in. Without haste Ben drove down to the ground level and worked his way out of the city. As he drove, April took the stolen jewels and watches from her bag and packed them in the small backpack. Once clear of Bridgeport Ben drove directly to Stamford. In a quiet residential neighborhood he stopped behind a green Ford sedan.

"See you tomorrow," he said as he got out, pulling a long black bag from under his seat and reaching for the backpack. April slid into the driver's seat without a word and drove away.

Ben loaded his two bags on the floor behind him, started the engine and left the area. At Norwalk he entered another multi-level car park and drove to the upper level where he parked the Ford in a corner stall. He tucked April's shotgun, still in its black bag, out of sight under the front seat. Depositing the keys in the glove compartment, he locked the car. Ballistics tests would later prove the shotgun found in the stolen Ford was almost certainly the weapon which had killed the jeweller in Lebanon. The police had a murder weapon – but no suspects, so far.

Four spaces away from the Ford, Ben unlocked a silver and black Bronco and got in. Sitting silently in the Mustang at the far end of the same aisle April watched until a puff of smoke from the Bronco's exhaust warned he was ready. She pulled forwards out of her spot as Ben backed out of his.

April left the parking lot three cars in front of Ben. Spaced well apart they followed Highway 95 to New York City. When April picked up the first signs for John F. Kennedy International Airport, Ben had already turned off for Yonkers. They both kept their speed constant. Neither was in a hurry.

April parked and locked Ben's Mustang and dropped her keys into a garbage bin. She checked in at the American Airlines counter a few minutes later with one bulging bag and one carry on. She accepted window seat 32A and wandered through security to the departure gate. She spoke to no one in the lounge and spent most of the overnight flight asleep. Her seat companions, an older couple on their way home to Lyon, left her to her own devices.

Ben's detour via Yonkers put him at JFK an hour and a half later than April. He parked the Bronco, found the Mustang, and retrieved the bag with all his clothes from the trunk. He tossed the keys to both vehicles as far as he could and set off for the Air France check-in counter. As April's TWA L-1011 climbed into the night sky over Long Island, Ben sat waiting patiently in his departure lounge. Outside a Boeing 747 in Air France livery was being loaded with freight pallets underneath and meals for the passengers through an upper door.

When her flight touched down at Charles De Gaulle Airport the following day April was wide awake and getting excited. Following Ben's instructions, she changed money before buying a ticket on the commuter train into Paris. At the designated station she got off and made her way to the streets above. Five minutes later she presented her prepaid voucher at the Hotel Suez and accepted her room key. Outside, on Boulevard St. Michel, it was raining hard.

Ben's trans-Atlantic flight arrived in Paris about the time his partner was stripping off her clothes for a shower in the hotel. Taking the same commuter train route as April, Ben reached the Hotel Suez in the late morning. The rain had stopped. The streets were drying and, occasionally, the sun managed to filter its way through slim breaks in the clouds. April was waiting for Ben wearing nothing but a thin bathrobe.

* * *

Rupert Allen and Charles Berglund were young, handsome, privileged, and crooked. They were con men. At Oxford they were often bored. There, in the cloistered world of the ancient university, surrounded by an urban population of mostly working-class families, they had been forced to make their own entertainment. Not ones to fraternize with the locals, apart from the occasional urgent coupling with tarty teens in tight sweaters, short skirts, and accents which strained the English language to dangerous limits, the pair took to exploration.

The roof tops of the 'City of Dreaming Spires' were fertile ground for two young men with the spirit of adventure in their blood. With similar backgrounds, both being from military families, the two evenly matched scholars were drawn to each other.

Rupert's great grandfather had served with Kitchener in the Sudan. His grandfather had led his troops successfully and, for him, safely, through the Great War. His father had served with distinction on Montgomery's North African staff in the 1939-1945 conflict and again, courageously, in Korea. Rupert was expected to follow in their illustrious footsteps and take up a career in the guards when he came down from Oxford with an honours degree in classics. He had no intention of doing so.

Charles was born among the American blue bloods of New Hampshire. He was a descendent of an aristocratic Swedish naval officer who had sailed with John Paul Jones during the American War of Independence. All first born sons, since that time, had served the US Navy with valour. From 1845 onwards all had been educated at Annapolis, the US Naval Academy. Charles was no exception. He even managed to earn a place on the football team and played in one Army versus Navy contest. Injuries eventually persuaded him to abandon the sport. Unlike his predecessors, Charles had gone directly from Annapolis to Oxford to read classics. Having experienced something of naval life he had no desire to see more.

Rupert was definitely a bad influence on Charles. Early in their first year at Oxford they were arrested for being drunk and disorderly on The High: a result of Rupert's desire to try what he referred to as 'the ultimate pub crawl.' From Carfax, in the centre of town, the plan was to have half a pint of bitter in every pub within a kilometre radius of the clock tower. They began their quest at seven that evening and were apprehended a few minutes before ten. They were fortunate that the police constable who discovered the pair trying to dance with a traffic light owned a well-developed sense of humour. He escorted them back to college and handed them over to the university authorities.

Rupert, reading Matthew Arnold one evening, found his mind returning over and over to one line - 'these are our young barbarians all at play.' He extended his playful horizons and came up with the idea of seeing just how far he and Charles could travel in one full night over the roof tops of the city. Excited by the success of their self-imposed mission, they went out night after night in different directions. For many weeks their nocturnal wanderings kept them occupied. Those expeditions led to successful climbs of the imposing domed facade of the Radcliffe Camera and the sheer exterior of Magdalen College tower.

After they came down from Oxford with their degrees, Charles went home for a while. The expected row with his father about his decision not to stay in the navy was noisy and protracted, as Charles had anticipated. He fled back to England with his distinguished tail between his legs. Rupert, who had experienced a similarly heated exchange with his own family, was dealing in antiques from a large, renovated farmhouse near Henley. He invited Charles to invest in the company and join him as a partner. The two were good at buying and selling antiques and so they prospered, but they were still bored. They needed something to help them recapture the excitement of their adventures at Oxford. Any form of military training for a future war was not the answer for them.

Rupert heard about the diamond first. A contact at Sotheby's told him about the impending auction in Geneva. A garish weekly magazine of show business and society gossip added a series of photographs of previous owners and a large portrait of current owner, Tango Perez, holding the gem in his hand. The article announced that the diamond was soon to be displayed in Antwerp for one week immediately prior to the sale. The report claimed the *Namib Star* was unlucky: misfortune befell anyone who came in contact with it.

The magazine erroneously reported that the *Namib Star* had only ever had four owners. A diamond dealer, Manfred Goldstein, it said, had found the rough gem in a desert in South West Africa. Following a lengthy process of cutting and polishing in Antwerp, Goldstein had sold the finished diamond, through an intermediary, to someone in New York. The identity of the second owner had not been revealed until after his death. His wife, once again through an intermediary, put the diamond back into circulation as 1949 came to a close.

A flamboyant Hollywood movie magnate purchased it in the early months of 1950 for a buxom starlet he then married. Two years later, after a spectacular flop of a movie, he dropped her and her contract. Never again did he make a successful film. Within five years he was dead, killed by depression and addiction to pills and alcohol.

His former wife sold the diamond to the only son of a Costa Rican nobleman. She used the proceeds to fund her own production company. As a producer she excelled. The company prospered, she even won an Academy Award. Sadly, she died of cancer before she was forty.

The diamond remained in the Costa Rican's possession for over four decades. By 1997 Antonio Carlos Riviero y Perez, last of a long line of dissident Spanish aristocracy with centuries of family history in Central America, was strapped for cash. Well into his sixties, the once lithe and handsome polo player was a corpulent balding caricature of his former self. With little left from a healthy legacy, after a lifetime of self-indulgence and failed businesses, he had no choice but to auction his most prized possession, the *Namib Star.*

Rupert was intrigued enough to look up more details of the diamond's history in an encyclopedia. He was more than a little impressed when he read the true facts. His fertile mind began to examine the possibility of assisting in an unexpected change of ownership. He showed Charles the magazine article with a flourish.

"Charles, old chap. I think we should go into the diamond business."

Charles read the information, tossed the magazine back to Rupert and said, "Oh sure, we'll just walk in and take it in front of a platoon of armed guards."

"No. Look it shows in this diagram how the diamond will be displayed on a low pedestal. Obviously there will be sensors on the pedestal and electronic surveillance all over the place. That doesn't make it impossible to steal."

"You're right. Not impossible, but damned close to it." Charles was not convinced. "Anyway," he added, "that diamond is said to be unlucky."

"Read the article again, my friend. The luck wasn't all bad. Most of the owners died of natural causes anyway."

Knowing Rupert so well, Charles had no doubt his partner had every intention of pursuing the idea. As usual, he went along for the ride. Once he'd made up his mind on a course of action, or someone had made it up for him, Charles threw his considerable mental and physical abilities into the project.

Rupert invited a trio of security specialists to visit the converted farmhouse on the pretext of purchasing an expensive electronic surveillance system. While Rupert studied the modern techniques necessary to protect their valuable stock, Charles spent hours in a reference library learning about other robberies – the failures as well as the successes.

A week later, Charles flew to Antwerp to reconnoitre the scene. Over two rainy days he alternated between wandering through the Heritage Diamond Museum, roaming the surrounding streets and observing the museum's staff. In a smoke-filled coffee bar and, later, in his hotel room, he typed his findings and opinions into his laptop computer.

"We need to find an actor. One who speaks Dutch as well as English preferably," he explained to Rupert on his return. "There's an old curator; he's been looking after the museum since it opened from the look of him. We need to replace him with our own man."

"You mean kidnap him?" Rupert raised his eyebrows sharply.

"Yeah, for a couple of days only. Then we release him unharmed." Charles leaned back against an antique corner cabinet, his hands in his blazer pockets. "All we need is someone to impersonate him, to get us in and then out safely with the diamond."

Rupert sat with his fingertips together touching his lips, his elbows on his knees. His right foot tapped a thoughtful rhythm on the floor. He looked up at Charles with a grin spreading over his face.

"I wonder if old Buckingham could help?" he mused. "Didn't he have ambitions to go on the stage?"

Charles nodded with delight. "That's a possibility. His family live in Oxford, let's give them a call and see where he is."

A long conversation with their former college associate gave them the answers they wanted. Rupert quickly converted his new-found knowledge into a list of theatrical agents. Most answered his questions politely, perhaps curiously, yet couldn't help. Two were rude enough to accuse him of wasting their time. One had the right answer. The actor they needed was currently appearing in a small theatre in the Midlands.

* * *

"Come on, Andy, don't be difficult. You know it will make a great centrepiece..." Nick Gradowski listened as his editor interrupted. Holding the phone away from his ear a little he raised his eyes in silent prayer before trying again.

"Andy. Andy. Listen to me a moment. We've discussed all this before. The Antwerp tourism people have already agreed to cover my accommodation and Trans International still owe me a ticket. All it's gonna cost you is my meals. And you know I'm too busy to eat properly most of the time."

"Okay, Nick, you win, but two weeks. D'ya hear me? You've still got that river rafting job to do before your contract runs out. Two weeks. That's all. Then you get your ass back here on the double. Understood?"

Nick looked out of his window at the snow-clad mountains behind Seattle and clenched his fist in delight. "I'll be back, Andy. Don't worry about that. And I'll bring you a spread to be proud of. Thanks, old buddy."

Nick Gradowski was thirty-three and single. He was a fraction over six feet tall with a slim athletic build. His light brown hair, unfashionably long, was tied back in a pony tail with an elastic band. He had been a professional photographer ever since he left high school. Starting as an assistant to a high-profile studio photographer, Nick had soaked up knowledge and learned his craft well. Rarely was he seen after that without a bulging camera bag hanging from his right shoulder. From the studio he'd gone on to the sports desk of a local newspaper for a couple of years. Finally, at a cocky twenty-three years, he took the ultimate gamble and went freelance. Since then his assignments had taken him to all continents and many countries. Well respected by editors and other photographers, Nick loved to travel with his cameras and film.

In a way, he still was a freelance. Nick preferred to be his own master. Although he worked for anyone who could pay, he liked to have what he called 'a couple of bread and butter jobs' on hand at all times. One of those was a contract for two years to supply one photographic feature each month for *High Style*, a glossy up-market consumer magazine. The diamond story would be one of the last of that series. As he put down the phone his dark brown eyes were shining.

"Antwerp, here I come," he sang.

* * *

Rupert and Charles sat in the centre of the third row. Around them many seats were empty. The theatre, on a Saturday night, was less than one third full. Shakespeare's *All's Well That Ends Well* was not high on the list of entertainments available in Birmingham that rainy evening.

Act IV, Scene III, was playing before Rupert finally identified the actor he wanted. Later, of course, after he met him face to face, he remembered seeing him in a number of guises in most of the play. A servant entered from stage left. The First Lord broke into his own discourse and asked, "How now! Where's your master?"

As the servant answered, "He met the Duke in...", Rupert nudged Charles. "That's him. I'm sure that's Montague."

The two sat patiently through the remaining act, waiting until the King had delivered his epilogue, finishing with the words, "...and take our hearts."

The King left the stage. The curtain dropped and a mad scramble ensued for the exit. When the curtain rose again for the cast to take their bows, few remained to applaud their efforts. At least half the audience were filing into the pub across the street.

Rupert and Charles went out and waited beside the stage door, their raincoat collars turned up against the drizzle. No one else showed any interest in meeting the acting cast. The actors came out singly and in pairs. They looked hopefully at the two soaked theatre fans, silently praying for one of them to ask for an autograph. They were all disappointed. Chris Montague, known to his family as Bob Smith, left the theatre by himself. With a duffel bag slung over his shoulder he looked up at the rain, swore and started across the street. Rupert called to him.

"Mister Montague. Do you have a moment please?" The voice was upper class and determined.

Chris, unable to believe these two could really be interested in him, especially on a night when it was pissing with rain, kept walking. Rupert and Charles ran after him.

"Mister Montague. We really would like to talk to you. Can we buy you a drink?"

"Leave me alone, please. Just because I'm in the theatre doesn't mean..."

"No. Nothing like that, I assure you," Charles spoke first, his cultured American voice sowing the first seeds of interest in Montague, "We have a business proposition for you."

"It's an acting job, actually," Rupert finished.

Montague stopped walking. "There's a coffee house around the corner, we'll go there."

Rupert and Charles exchanged glances, knowing Montague was hooked. Now they just had to land him and hold on to him for a few weeks.

While they waited for their Cappucini in the coffee bar, the two Oxford University graduates introduced themselves and complimented the actor on his performance. Chris doubted they had taken much notice of him, still, he reasoned, at least they knew their Shakespeare well enough to discuss the play intelligently. His eyes flicked from one to the other as they talked.

The American was tall and blond, his hair a little long, curling on his broad shoulders, his eyes blue. When he smiled, which he did easily, he showed perfect white teeth. Chris noticed a slight ridge along the left side of Berglund's jaw, as if it had been broken at some time and not set properly. His nose wasn't quite straight either. Perhaps he had been an amateur boxer, Chris decided. Rupert Allen, by contrast, was dark haired, almost as tall, but slimly built. His brown eyes gleamed while he spoke of his own love of the classics of literature, particularly Shakespeare.

"I quite enjoyed my limited forays into amateur dramatics at school, and at Oxford, you know. Particularly liked playing Macbeth for some reason."

"When does this play close?" Charles broke in.

"Tonight. That's it. We're finished. Back on the dole for most of us. Until another part comes up."

Rupert smiled warmly. "Not for you, Chris. If you are interested, you could be in Belgium tomorrow with a guaranteed two to three week's work, for which we'll pay a month's wages, cash in advance."

Chris was interested. A job was a job. Any job would do at the moment, he reflected. The contents of his pockets held his total wealth: £15.70. His small part in the recently finished play would not add much more.

"What do you want me to do?"

"Can we go somewhere more private?" Rupert suggested, "We're staying at the Landmark Hotel, let's go there and we'll give you all the details."

In the spacious hotel suite, Charles ordered drinks from room service. The three sat in comfortable arm chairs, a coffee table between them.

Chris picked up his scotch and water, "Cheers." He took a large swallow and sat back, the glass in his hand. "Okay, gentlemen, would you please tell me what this is all about?"

"We want you to study an old man in Antwerp. It's really as simple as that. Once you have mastered his every move, we want you to become him, for approximately two days."

Chris looked at the two long and hard. "I get the impression there's something a little illegal in this enterprise." He said it slowly, enunciating each word carefully. He made it sound like a statement.

Rupert and Charles looked at each other. There was a long pause. "Yes, a little," Charles answered with a half smile.

"How little? And what's the risk to me?"

"Actually, we're planning to steal one of the most expensive diamonds in the world," Rupert told Chris modestly. "It's said to be worth ten million pounds."

"You two are out of your fucking minds," Chris exploded. "You're planning to steal a diamond worth ten million quid. And what, exactly, do you expect me to do to help?"

"As I told you; learn to be a particular old man in Antwerp and then replace him for two days. That's all."

"What happens if I get caught? I could spend the rest of my life in prison."

"You won't get caught," Rupert promised soothingly. "If there are any risks to be taken, we'll take them, not you."

Chris got up and paced the room for a few minutes, his brow furrowed. He swung back to Rupert.

"What's in it for me?"

"You get half a million pounds when the diamond is sold."

"Are you serious? Half a million?" Chris's face went white. "How do I know you'll pay up?"

"You don't. You'll simply have to trust us, old boy."

"There's a wonderful offer, a chance to put my trust in a couple of common thieves," Chris's voice dripped sarcasm as he looked from one to the other. Neither seemed overly concerned at the reaction, although Rupert had frowned almost imperceptibly at the use of the adjective 'common.'

"And if I say, no, to your generous offer. What then?"

"Perhaps we'll have to tell the police about the grass in your flat, and all those funny little tablets." Charles stood up as he spoke, a hint of menace in his voice. "And with your prior conviction..." he left the sentence hanging.

"You bastards." Chris rubbed his eyes with his fingers, feeling the sting of angry tears. "You bastards. You've been in my flat?" He glared at them with distaste. "And I wasn't convicted, only cautioned. Why me? There are hundreds of actors who could do this. Why pick on me?"

"I should think it's quite obvious, old chap," Rupert poured the words like oil. "Antwerp is in Flanders where most people speak three or four languages. Flemish or Dutch being spoken by everyone. You, I know, have a Dutch mother. You've lived and worked in Holland and you speak the language fluently."

"You're no Macbeth. You should have been playing Machiavelli at university."

Rupert ignored Chris's sudden interruption. "You are our first choice and our only choice. The fascinating part is that you, dear boy, have no choice."

108

Chris sat with his eyes cast down, apparently studying his shoes. He wiped one toe cap against the back of his trouser leg. Slowly he looked up, meeting Rupert's amused smile.

"Are you sure there's no risk?"

"Positive old chap. Nothing at all to worry about."

"I'll need a couple of days to think about it. I'm not sure..."

"Oh, you'll say yes, you really don't have a choice you know, do you?" Rupert oozed confidence. "Two days, that's all. Call us at this number." He held out an embossed business card.

"See yourself out will you, there's a good chap."

Chris wandered deep in thought through the rain. He had one more night in the bed and breakfast house he and the rest of the cast used, before taking the bus back to London in the morning. He would be glad to get home, he could think more clearly in his own flat. Basically a shy, rather timid, and lonely person, Chris only showed his full mettle when on stage. The two men who had propositioned him frightened him more than he cared to admit.

One day later, in his own home, with his feet up on his worn and comfortable couch and a mug of tea in his hand, Chris thought about the offer. In truth he had thought of little else since he left Birmingham. The more he considered the idea the more it scared him. He was bright enough to recognize that the challenge also appealed to his professional side. He knew he could refuse. There was little chance that Rupert or Charles would report the dope in his flat. He could make things very difficult for them if they did. As a safety factor, he emptied the grass and the ecstasy tablets down the toilet. He watched with a glum expression as they chased each other round and round the whirlpool, faster and faster, before vanishing with a gurgling, sucking sigh into the sewers below.

For hours Chris argued the project back and forth between himself and his alter ego. The actor, who lived for the stage, no matter how insignificant the part, and the careful loner, whose only real vice was taking occasional drugs to carry him through the solitude his shyness created, were of widely different opinions. The idea of taking over someone's life, of living it for two days, of being that person in every detail, appealed to his actor's mentality.

"The perfect part for me. I can do it. I can do it," he hummed to himself.

Despite his building enthusiasm for the job, the quiet, rather nervous, young man, who lived alone because he preferred it, was concerned at the possibility of getting caught.

"You could spend half your life in prison if it goes wrong," he reminded the actor's ego.

On the floor at his feet a couple of bold lines across the pages of an open magazine caught his eye.

"The risk is the reward!"

Chris scanned the first few lines. The story was about a solo Antarctic adventurer eloquently explaining his attraction to dangerous endeavours.

"The risk is the reward," Chris repeated out loud. "I like that. The risk is the reward. It's true. Plus I'll get half a million quid if we succeed. Can't lose, can I?"

He had selected a mental one-way street, a cul-de-sac. The only way out was to back up, now. Before his nerve failed him, he dialed the number he had been given.

Charles answered with a polite, "Berglund Allen Antiques, good afternoon."

"Hello, it's Chris Montague. Okay, I'll do it. When do you want me to go?"

"That's fine, Chris, you won't regret it. I'll send a courier over with your instructions; your tickets and money for expenses. You can leave tomorrow. See you in Antwerp."

* * *

Paris suited April. It felt rich, looked elegant, sophisticated, everything she aspired to be. It was a world away from Buffalo. Two days after they arrived, Ben found them a small furnished apartment in the Latin Quarter, only five minutes' walk from the Hotel Suez. While April went sightseeing, on foot most of the time. Ben soon made himself known among the North African community, spending long hours in the first few days building contacts and a certain amount of credibility. As in the States, he gave his occupation as teacher. He let it be known that, politically, he was an Algerian first and a French resident second.

While Ben spent his time arguing the political situation in Algeria, April's perambulations took her to all the historic sights. From the apartment to Notre Dame Cathedral was a leisurely ten-minute walk. Notre Dame to the Arc de Triomphe, along the Champs Elysees, took her an hour. Much of that time was spent window shopping. Another half an hour saw her pass the imposing Palais de Chaillot and across the Seine to the Eiffel Tower. As she walked, April made careful note of her surroundings. She identified one-way streets and marked them as such on her map. Potential obstructions, such as traffic lights, road repairs, congested routes, were also marked. She highlighted jewellery shops with a pink marker pen.

April rode the elevator to the upper level of the Eiffel Tower surrounded by an excited crowd of teenage American tourists. For a long time she stood there silently, looking out over the city with a mixture of childish enthusiasm and professional interest. Around her the school group pushed noisily from corner to corner. April ignored them, deep in her own thoughts, already planning her next robberies. She took her time coming down, taking the open stairs and stopping regularly to absorb the view. April was almost ready to go back to work, after a few more sightseeing walks.

One evening April tried to persuade Yusuf, one of Ben's new Algerian friends, to find her a gun.

"We always carry a gun at home in the States, for protection, you know," she lied, "everyone does it. I don't feel comfortable in a big city without one."

"I don't think you need one in Paris," Ben argued. "It's not exactly New York, is it?"

"I need one," April narrowed her eyes at Ben in warning. Smiling warmly, suggestively, at his friend she begged him to help.

"I'll see what I can do. No promises though," Yusuf smiled in reply.

Yusuf was, officially, the manager of his brother's restaurant. His extra-curricular activities included disposing of stolen property, small time arms dealer and political activist.

While Ben was shopping for a used car the next morning, his supposed friend learned just how far a determined girl would go to get what she wanted. April serviced Yusuf on her knees at his office desk. By the time she left he would have provided her with a complete arsenal if she had but asked. Three days later, while Ben was picking up his car, April received her gun. Ben was furious. Yusuf couldn't stop smiling.

"So, Ben. Where's the car? Show me. I want to see it." April tucked the pistol into her purse, linked her arm through Ben's and headed for the door. "Come on. Show me the car."

Out on the street, in front of the restaurant, stood Ben's French car. April was not impressed.

"What the fuck is that," she asked, pointing with distaste at the strange shape in front of her. "It looks like a tin can on wheels."

"It's a two CV, a Deux Chevaux, they're famous."

"Yeah, more like rent-a-wreck for a buck. I'm not riding in that shit-box."

It took Ben the rest of the day to convince April that no one in France would think she was strange, or poor, if she had a Deux Chevaux.

"Don't forget," he reminded her, "we need to fit in here. We need to be like everyone else."

April snorted in derision but she eventually went for a ride anyway. That jaunt did nothing to endear her to the vehicle. On two consecutive days, Ben used the 2CV to scout for a likely getaway car. April was getting restless. The only way to keep her happy was to start working again.

A holdup in Bercy was their first in Paris. It was also badly timed. April chose the location. It was also her choice to dress 'up market,' as she liked to call her favourite style of disguise. Ben decided on the method of attack. Neither of them knew anything about the funeral procession of thirty-seven cars scheduled to pass the jewellers while April was inside.

The shop was on a five-way corner, perfect for a getaway under normal circumstances. Ben parked his stolen Renault Nevada wagon right outside the jewellers, facing the multiple escape routes. He stayed at the wheel with the engine running. As April walked into the shop two motorcycle policemen, with sirens off but blue lights flashing, pulled to a halt in the middle of the intersection. The two dismounted and stopped all traffic. Parked illegally, Ben froze. Fervently he prayed April wasn't too busy to see what was happening.

A flower be-decked silver and black hearse, preceded by two more police motorcyclists, cruised sedately past. A convoy of cars filled with solemn faced mourners followed in dignified procession. Ben kept his eyes on the two motorcycle policemen, willing April to stay in the shop.

April caught the wink of a blue light as she pretended to examine a tray of rings. Moving further into the jewellers, away from the window, she asked to look at a diamond necklace. The price tag stated 39,000 Francs. April held the strand up to her throat as she mentally calculated the value in dollars. "Nearly seven thousand bucks," she thought.

"Oui," April spoke softly to muffle her atrocious accent, "Je prends ça."

Reaching into her over-sized purse, as if for her wallet, April's fingers wrapped around the grip of her pistol. Something in the change of expression, perhaps a hardening around her eyes, betrayed April's intentions. The jeweller, who had been robbed before, leaned forward with hand outstretched to grab April's wrist. He was too slow. April whipped the gun up hard and crashed it into the side of his head. Stunned and bleeding, a universe of stars exploding in his brain, the jeweller slumped to the floor. April took his keys and unlocked three cabinets. Hurriedly she filled her bag with rings, watches, and necklaces, including the first one she had chosen. On the floor the injured jeweller groaned weakly without moving. April nudged him with the toe of her shoe. He groaned again.

"Suffer, you stupid bastard," without thinking, April spoke loudly in English. Placing the gun in the pocket of her camel

113

coloured coat, she opened the cash register and looted the till. On the wall, close to the ceiling above her, a miniature camera recorded every movement she and the jeweller made. Unfortunately it couldn't see much outside: except indistinct outlines through the glass. The last of the funeral cars passed Ben. The two policemen mounted their bikes, waved the stationary traffic into motion, and sped off in pursuit of the cortege. April sauntered calmly from the shop and got in beside her partner.

"Let's go, Sugar," she smiled.

Ben eased into the traffic and turned right. "Everything okay?" he asked.

April nodded. "Sure, I had to give him a little tap on the head as a warning, but he's fine."

"What did you get?"

"The usual, some good stuff. And the till was full of cash too. Don't often see that these days. I took the lot."

"Any cameras?"

"What d'ya want a camera for?"

"Not for me, stupid. Were there any security cameras?"

April looked at him in horror. "Oh fuck! I forgot to look."

"You'd better get changed quickly and take the Metro home. Wait for me at Yusuf's. I'll get rid of the car."

April stripped off the long, curly blonde wig. Out came the contact lenses. She pulled off her skirt and struggled into a pair of jeans. The camel coloured coat went into a plastic bag and was tucked under her seat. She replaced it with a dark blue windbreaker, zipping it up to cover her chocolate brown sweater. Stylish shoes went into the side pocket on her door. Quickly she laced up her old Doc Martens. The she stuffed her big her purse with the takings into a small backpack and placed the gun on top.

"Okay, Ben. I'm ready."

The transformation from well-dressed shopper to casual teenager had taken less than two minutes. Ben pointed to a railway station entrance ahead.

"That's the Gare de Lyon. There's a Metro entrance there as well. See you in about an hour."

Without a word April got out and walked away with her hands in her pockets. Her nonchalance made her all but invisible among the other pedestrians. Ben drove carefully across the bridge over the Seine to Gare d'Austerlitz. There, in a side street, he double parked the Renault beside another station wagon in front of his 2CV. He switched cars and contents without anyone noticing anything out of the ordinary. Confident everything had gone well, he drove back to the Latin Quarter where he parked in a lane behind the restaurant. Locking the car, Ben opened the back door and made his way through a kitchen, smelling the spicy African cooking with pleasure. He opened the door to a small office. April was already there, sipping on a beer. Yusuf was with her. April's bag was tucked on the floor between them. Ben reached down and picked it up.

"Have you seen any of it yet?" he looked at Yusuf but nodded towards April.

"He's seen it. He'll take it. All of it, except one necklace, which I'm keeping," April interjected.

"Hold it, April," Ben warned. "You don't keep anything, that's the rules."

"Up yours, Ben," April sneered back. "I'm keepin' it and there's nothin' you can do about it."

Ben clenched his fists and glared at his partner. "You're not keeping anything. Understand? Nothing."

He took a step forward and stopped as the business end of April's pistol pointed at his chest.

"I said, I'm keepin' it, Ben. I stole it. I'm keepin' it."

"Put the gun down, April and be smart. If you keep anything the cops will catch us one day for sure. Everything goes. Got that?"

April slowly shook her head, "Not this time, buddy. I'm keepin' it."

Yusuf watched the exchange with interest, without expression on his face. His eyes flicked from April to Ben and back again. April hadn't moved. She kept the pistol trained on Ben's chest. He looked at Yusuf as if for support. All he got in return was a slight shake of the head.

"Put the gun down, April or I'll..."

"You'll do what?" she interrupted. "You gonna throw a punch? Fuck, you'll be dead before you take one more step."

Ben pointed his finger at her, his arm trembling. "You're crazy, you know that? You're fucking well crazy."

Turning his back on the gun Ben passed over the robbery spoils, minus the diamond necklace, to Yusuf. He received a sheaf of notes in exchange.

"We'll pay you the rest when it's all sold," Yusuf said. His voice dripped ice. If Ben was disappointed he didn't show it. He was more concerned at his loss of face. April nodded with satisfaction and put the pistol away. She finished her beer as Ben counted the notes.

"Okay, that's okay," he told Yusuf. "I'm happy to get the rest later."

Ben and April missed the first edition of the news that night. They were too busy with April's post robbery stripping ritual. The only item April kept on was a glittering diamond necklace. Ben was furious but managed not to comment.

The late news repeated the story of the robbery of a jewellery store in Bercy. The proprietor, it stated, had suffered a fractured skull after being clubbed with a gun. Paris police were said to be looking for a smartly dressed woman in her early thirties. She was believed to have long, blonde curly hair and to be wearing a camel coloured coat. A police spokesman offered the opinion she might, possibly, be an American. She was thought to have an accomplice driving a black, late model Renault Nevada station wagon. Nothing more was known.

"I thought you only gave him a tap," Ben whined. "You've got to be more careful, April, this is Paris, not Buffalo."

"He shoulda kept his hands to himself. He asked for it."

"And keep your mouth shut next time," Ben warned. "Now they know you're American. There must have been a camera in there."

"They know nuthin. They just think they know, that's all. I ain't got long, blonde curly hair."

After Ben fell asleep, April hid the necklace in the bottom of a full carton of tampons. Ben would never think of looking for it there, she reasoned.

The next day the pair hit another small jeweller in Clichy, not far from the Pet Cemetery by the bridge. This time April was in and out in less than forty seconds. She wore a long, black wig, clear glasses, black gloves, and a black raincoat. More aware of danger after Bercy, she saw the camera without looking directly at it. The camera, ever watchful, supposedly all seeing, only picked up a fraction of a second of the image of April's profile. It was almost enough.

In a conscious effort to be as unpredictable as possible, April changed clothes rapidly in their stolen car only one block from the robbery. Ben drove the car away by himself while April, once again looking like a sprightly teenager, wandered down to the Seine.

Two streets away Ben parked the getaway vehicle illegally across a driveway clearly marked 'Stationement Interdit.' Leaving the keys in the ignition, he walked without haste the one block to where he had parked his own car. April's disguise, tucked into a plastic bag marked *Chantelle*, hung loosely from his right hand. Looking perplexed Ben walked the length of the street twice, studying each of the cars on both sides of the road. His car was missing.

"Fuck it. Fuck it. Fuck it," he shouted. A passerby looked at him in surprise and gave the angry young man plenty of room.

April sat on a brick wall watching the river traffic. Occasionally she glanced back to the road. Ben was taking longer than expected. Half an hour went by. April started to get concerned. A nagging doubt preyed on her mind. Was it possible that Ben had taken off without her?

While she waited and wondered, April chewed on a thumb nail. She was getting nervous. Without Ben she had nothing, except the latest proceeds. He took care of all the money. Yusuf, she knew, would never pay her as much as he paid Ben. Not even if she added herself to the bargain. She waited another few minutes wondering what to do.

Across the street a familiar scrawny figure took his life in his hands and threw himself towards her. Dodging from left to right he made it through the traffic without getting hit. He still carried the *Chantelle* bag.

"Where the fuck have you been?" April screamed. "I've been worried sick about you."

"Someone stole our fucking car," Ben wailed. "They stole my fucking car."

In spite of her earlier concern April found it impossible not to smile.

"What the fuck are you smirking at? You stupid bitch."

April, unable to hold her amusement any longer, burst out laughing and slid off the wall.

"Why the fuck would anyone want to steal that pile of junk?"

Ben slapped her hard across the face, snarling, "Don't laugh at me, you whore."

April stopped abruptly. She bunched both her fists and took a step forward. Ben stood his ground.

"You got that, April? Don't ever laugh at me again." The words came out through gritted teeth.

"Fuck you. You jerk. Now go and steal another car, so we can go home." April had the last word as usual.

"I'll get one tomorrow. Let's walk a bit, I need to think."

Keeping a pace or two apart they followed the wall fifty metres or so to an ornate iron gate.

"Hey, Ben, what's this place?"

Ben read the inscription with interest, "It's a pet cemetery. You know, where people bury dogs and cats."

"Bullshit. You're kidding me. Let's go look."

Ben paid the few francs admission and followed an awestruck April into the beautifully laid out gardens. Watched by Ben, April frowned as she tried to decipher the French inscription on a monument to a St. Bernard. Her lips moved as she silently spoke the words, some of which she knew, most she didn't.

"What's it say, Sugar? You read it to me."

"It says, this is Barry. He saved forty people's lives and died trying to rescue the forty-first. That was way back in 1814."

118

"No shit, Ben. Did he really?"

"I guess so. That's what it says."

Ben took her by the hand, "Come on, Rin Tin Tin's buried here too."

For an hour the two jewel thieves forgot about rings and watches, security cameras, police, and stolen cars. Excitedly April, who had never owned a pet, rushed from grave to grave.

"Look at this one, Sugar, it says something about, uh, humans and, uh, something by my dog."

"Dèçue par les humains, jamais par mon chien," Ben read. "That means; disappointed by humans, never by my dog."

"Great," April's eyes were shining, "that's great. Can we get a dog, Sugar?"

"Don't be fucking stupid, April. What would we do with a dog? Come on, let's get outta here."

All the way to Yusuf's restaurant, on foot part way and by Metro the rest, April badgered Ben about getting a dog.

"What are we gonna do with a dog?" he complained.

"I'll look after it and feed it and take it for walks. I promise."

"Sure you will."

"I will, I promise."

Ben agreed to think about it, "In a few weeks when we get a decent place to live."

April hugged him, her anger at being slapped forgotten for the moment. The idea of owning a dog excited her. It would be something warm and cuddly, something of her very own.

That night, while Ben pumped and grunted on top of her, April slowly reached one hand under her pillow. She pulled out her pistol, rammed it against Ben's temple and cocked it in one fluid motion.

"Don't ever hit me again, you son of a bitch, or I'll blow your fuckin' head off."

Ben stopped immediately and opened his eyes in horror, "Put it away, April. This is not a game."

"You're fuckin' right, Ben. This is NO fuckin' game," April shouted, pushing the gun harder. April felt Ben's erection wither and die inside her. She kept the gun tight against his head.

"You got that, Sugar? You understand what I'm saying? Hit me again and I'll smear your brains all over the fuckin' wall. Now get that useless limp prick outta me."

April rolled out from under Ben's sagging body and stood up. She pointed the gun at him again. "Don't ever. Okay?"

"You're crazy, you know that? You're fucking crazy," Ben screamed as he struggled into his pants.

"Yeah, so you told me." April sat down on the couch, still smiling, still pointing the gun at him as he dressed.

"Now go get us some beer, Sugar. I'll make it up to you when you get back."

Ben grabbed a handful of change from a night table and fled. No matter how he tried he could not get used to April's dangerous and unexpected mood swings. When he plucked up the courage to return hours later April was in bed and asleep. Ben crawled in beside her after making sure the gun was no longer under her pillow. April stirred.

"It's okay, Sugar. I wouldn't really hurt you," she ran her hand down to his crotch as she whispered in the darkness. "Now, let's wake this little boy up and turn him into a man."

* * *

Nick Gradowski watched the girl discreetly over his coffee cup as she walked towards him across the sunlit, cobblestone square. She was not tall but, in high heels, she looked it. Her frame was large for a woman, though well proportioned, with a figure to turn men's heads. Nick's eyes flicked to slim ankles and up to shapely calves. Above her knees her sun-tanned thighs disappeared into a short, blood red dress. She tossed her lion's mane of fair, fluffy curls and lifted the hair off the back of her neck with one hand. Dangling almost to her shoulders a pair of hooped golden earrings glinted in the sunlight. She turned to look at the cathedral clock, her grey eyes wandering over the outdoor restaurant tables.

With no more than a glance at Nick, she sat at a table to his left. She pulled a notebook and ball point pen from her purse and began scribbling rapidly. 'Clear complexion. Hair too long but clean and tidy. Beige buckskin jacket with long fringes on shoulders and sleeves. Blue denim shirt and jeans. Lightweight green and brown hiking boots. Good looking man, probably about 30. American or Canadian? Eyes?'

Nick leaned back in his chair and swung his gaze round the square, letting it linger on the girl a few seconds longer than necessary. He nodded to himself in approval. Unusually for a big girl, he thought, she looked good in a short skirt. To Nick's practiced eye she was deliciously raunchy and sexy. Out of the corner of his eye he studied her more closely. Her finger nails were painted silvery white. The hands were long and well cared for. Peeping from her open toe shoes a set of bright red nails matched her dress.

A waiter blocked Nick's view for a moment to take her order. In rapid Flemish, which Nick found impossible to comprehend, he gave her a list of options. In a voice which, Nick guessed, owed much to the upper echelons of the British school system she ordered tea, with a slice of lemon. She ordered in English, as Nick had done.

Nick let out a long breath and began whistling softly. This, he decided, was no ordinary English rose. No sir. Not just a rose. She was the whole damn bush. With movements born of long practice, he reached under the table and pulled a camera from his bag. Holding it on his lap he pressed the shutter. She noticed the slight click and looked in his direction, her head a little on one side. A quizzical smile on her face.

"Oops," said Nick, "you caught me. I'm just playing candid camera. I hope you don't mind?" He raised his eyebrows to show it was a friendly question.

The girl smiled again and shook her head. "No, that's fine. I don't mind." She had a gentle voice, a trifle husky. A bit like sudden laughter. Nick noticed she wore a thin veneer of green eye-liner. It complimented her eyes and her dress. She went back to her notes. Nick continued to watch her, openly this time, with his elbow on the table and his chin resting on one hand.

"What's your name?" he asked.

"Why?" She wrote two words 'dark brown,' closed her notebook and faced him. "Are you trying to pick me up?"

Nick laughed out loud, causing a few others within hearing to break their conversations momentarily and look up. "Yes, I think I am. May I join you?"

She nodded, smiling, confident and unafraid with so many people around. Nick picked up his camera bag and his drink and flowed to her table in one smooth motion.

"Hi, I'm Nick Gradowski," he held out his hand and shook hers once.

"Sam. Samantha actually. Samantha Walker. Are you American?"

"Yep. I'm from Seattle, Washington. On the west coast. You're English, right?"

"Yes, from Oxford."

"Are you..." they both started together and laughed. "Go ahead," Nick suggested.

"Are you on holiday?"

"No, I'm a magazine photographer. I'm here to do a photo spread on the diamond industry. I just arrived yesterday. And you?"

Sam held up her notebook, "That's great, I'm a freelance writer. I'm here to research a feature on the Flemish masters."

"Maybe we can help each other. Do the guys at the tourist office know you're here? They're real helpful. They gave me a load of useful contacts."

"I don't think I need help really. The photography for my feature has already been done by somebody else," Sam stopped, her journalist's mind taking up the slack. "What's the focus of your spread, if you'll excuse the obvious pun?"

"Basically, it's a piece on the diamond industry today. I've already contacted a Belgian expert on the subject to write the article. Why do you ask?"

"Look, I don't mean to be forward, and don't get the wrong idea," Sam leaned forward anyway, her ample chest resting on the table. Nick tried to keep his eyes on Sam's face. For some reason gravity made them droop a few degrees.

"Do you know there's a fantastic diamond due to go on display here at a museum in a few days' time? It's supposed to be unlucky. It sounds exciting. Why don't we team up and do another feature on its history?" Sam stopped again trying to look a little embarrassed. "Sorry, I get carried away sometimes. I'm always looking for ways to double my income on each job."

Nick laughed. "Yeah, I know how that feels. I heard about the diamond last night. I'm hoping to get permission to photograph it before the public are allowed in the first day. I'll see if I can get you in too. You do have a press card, don't you?"

Sam rummaged in her huge purse and came up with a laminated card. "Tra Laa!"

Nick looked at his watch. "I have an appointment, I have to go. Where are you staying?"

"I'm at the Renaissance Hotel."

"Good, I'm just around the corner at the Columbus. I'll leave a message for you early this evening."

Sam's tea had gone cold while they talked so she asked for another one. Seeing the waiter with a tray of sugary cakes she ordered one for herself. She never could resist anything sweet. Sam sat thinking about Nick as she devoured her snack. She thought she had seen his work in a couple of adventure magazines. Those features were on outdoor pursuits. Static diamonds were quite a change from action photography. It seemed that Nick, like herself, had few subject limitations when it came to getting a story. On an impulse she pulled out her cell phone and called London.

"Hi, Trish, it's Sam. Yes, I'm in Antwerp. Oh, it's beautiful and, surprise, the sun's shining." For a few minutes they chattered back and forth. "Trish, what do you know about an American photographer named Nick Gradowski? Have you heard of him?"

"Yes, of course I have. He's good. In fact, I'm using one of his pics on next month's front cover. We buy his stock photography from Optimum Lens Photo Library. They have an office in New York too. Why do you want to know?"

Sam recounted the discussion with Nick.

"Go for it, Sam. It sounds like a great story and let me see it first. Gradowski is the perfect photographer to shoot diamonds. His ability with lighting is amazing. Nick is meticulous in everything he does. You'll make a great team. And be careful of that diamond, I've heard it's unlucky. And watch the photographer. I hear he's a bit of a lady's man."

Sam laughed, "Okay, Trish, thanks. I'll be careful, I promise." She rang off and put the phone in her bag. On a fresh page in her notebook she wrote *Namib Star* and underlined it. She jotted a page of notes, thoughts, questions to ask and possible reference sources. If Nick did call her later she would tap his knowledge. For now a visit to the local newspaper was the natural first move. As she walked away, past the statue of Sir Pieter Paul Rubens standing on its pedestal in the middle of Groenplaats, he seemed to frown at her as if to ask, "What about my story, young lady?"

Nick took the Metro tram from Groenplaats Station to Opera. Coming up on to de Keyserlei, across from the modern Antwerp Tower, he strode the cobblestones straight to the diamond district. On Hoveniersstraat he entered a tall, grey building and took the elevator to the sixth floor. The door opened to show racks of filing cabinets ahead and a small waiting area to his right. The two empty chairs and a small table with a vase of flowers and a few magazines were not inviting. To his left two open doors showed promise. An elderly lady looked up from a desk in one and asked a question in Flemish.

"Hi, I'm looking for Ingrid Strauss. I have an appointment with her," Nick replied with his usual disarming smile.

A voice from the next open door called out in slightly accented English, "Hello, Mr. Gradowski? I'm Ingrid Strauss."

A slim, stunningly attractive blonde, about twenty-five years old and no taller than his shoulder, stood in the doorway looking up at him. Wearing dark grey trousers and a crisp white cotton blouse with a diamond brooch on the collar, she looked efficient and, as far as Nick was concerned, extremely desirable. Ingrid held out her hand, her welcoming smile showing perfect white teeth. Nick grinned at her, clasped the hand briefly and let go.

"Hi. I'm here to take photos of the diamond process. You told me to come and see you first." He pulled a letter out of his inside pocket and held it out.

"Yes, I know. Everything is arranged. Marie will take you through the polishing and cutting areas today. Perhaps when you finish you will come back here. I will have some more contacts for you then." Ingrid passed Nick over to an older woman who turned on her heel with the order "Come!" Nick did as he was told.

For the next four hours Nick worked his way through the various stages in the processing of a diamond. The cutters and polishers knew he was there, though he did his best to stay in the background. Only the occasional bursts of flash were vivid reminders of his presence. Often he stood for long moments watching a process before raising his camera. A razor thin phosphor bronze saw blade cutting a diamond with infinite slowness held his attention.

"How fast is that blade spinning?" he asked a supervisor quietly.

"Fifteen thousand rpm. The blade is coated with a mixture of diamond powder and oil. It only cuts about two millimetres each hour. It's a very slow job."

Nick extended the legs of his tripod and aimed a lens at the point where the blade and diamond met. Setting the lens to its smallest aperture, he checked the light and set a time exposure. The supervisor watched Nick as he worked, changing camera settings every few frames until he was satisfied.

After taking a series of overall shots, to show the scope of the cutting and polishing room, Nick zoomed in close on a girdling machine. A diamond, no bigger than a match head, spun at the end of a wooden spindle, called a dop, attached to the chuck of a lathe. Pressed against it was another diamond, also held in a long wooden dop. One diamond turning against the other created the rounded, conical, base. Nick could see the diamond powder drifting into a small reservoir to be collected and used again.

"Doesn't anything get wasted around here?" Nick asked the machine operator.

"Not if it's part of a diamond."

"What happens if one of those diamonds jumps off the machine and is lost on the floor?" Nick turned to the taciturn Marie, his eyebrows raised in question and one finger pointing at the diamond.

"All doors lock electronically, immediately. No one is allowed to leave until it is found."

"Wow. That could be interesting. Imagine you and me locked in here together," Nick teased, flashing a broad grin at her. Marie kept a straight face and ignored him.

One elderly man, a polisher, studied a hand-drawn sketch on his bench. The drawing, of an emerald shaped diamond, showed what the finished stone would look like. Already the diamond was clamped in an adjustable dop and pressed to the surface of a spinning horizontal disc. Nick focused on the complete unit. The polisher was at work on the first of four main facets, or plane surfaces. Highlights glinting on the disc suggested more diamond dust in use. Nick shot a number of representative shots of the operation. Then he played artfully with his filters and lights, catching the dust and the diamond working together in a harmony of prismatic colours.

Nick shot ten rolls of film on three different cameras before he was satisfied he had the processes covered from all angles. If there was any problem he could easily return to re-shoot one or more aspects.

"Okay, Marie," Nick grinned at his guide, "I'm done. You can take me home now."

Marie wordlessly escorted him back to Ingrid's office and left him with a curt nod of her head.

"Talkative, isn't she?" Nick commented after Marie had gone.

"She's just shy," Ingrid answered with a half smile. "She's not used to Americans."

Nick laughed as he pulled out a notebook. "That explains everything. Now then, Ingrid, I've got a pile of questions for you."

For over an hour Nick plied Ingrid with a series of questions about the work of the Diamond Council and the important personalities. Who should he meet? Who should he photograph? Who would be of interest in the story? She answered the business questions efficiently, adding potential sources of further information. Nick finished by aiming a few personal ones at Ingrid as well.

A cheeky, "Do you have a man in your life?" went unanswered but was rewarded with a smile as Ingrid instinctively reached up a hand and checked her long hair.

"Why don't we have dinner together one night?"

The conversation quickly became like a fencing match. Two equals jabbing questions and answers at each other. A bystander might have thought the couple had known each other for a long time, they handled each other's words so well.

Two other girls at desks outside the office giggled quietly together as Nick asked his questions in a broad western accent. The open door to Ingrid's office made it easy for them to hear almost every word.

Ingrid told Nick she was leaving her job at the end of the month. "I'm going travelling for a year with a friend," she explained. "I want to see as much of the world as possible. Including America."

Nick smiled and played along, his voice loud and clear. "Well, if you come to Seattle, be sure and give me a call. I'd love to show you around, we have a few rough diamonds there too."

Ingrid looked puzzled for a second. "Thank you, maybe I will. Now, I have made an appointment for you to photograph a selection of finished diamonds tomorrow morning. Please be here at nine o'clock."

Nick was about to leave when he remembered his offer to Sam. "Oh, Ingrid. There's a writer here from England. She has an assignment to write about the Flemish painters. We'd like to team up and do a feature together on the *Namib Star*. Can you get her an invitation for the same time as I take the photographs?"

Ingrid frowned and stared at Nick for a second or two in apparent surprise. "Yes, I think so. I can try, anyway," she looked at Nick quizzically. "Tell her to bring her press card and passport to the office tomorrow."

"Thanks, Ingrid, I'll see you in the morning."

As soon as Nick reached his hotel he arranged with the concierge to send his films to a lab for processing.

"Tell them I need them back, unmounted, by tomorrow afternoon."

Once in his room, he phoned Sam. She answered on the fourth ring. "Samantha Walker speaking."

"Hi, Sam, this is Nick. What are you doing for dinner tonight? I think we should talk about our angle on this diamond job."

"Alright, I've nothing planned. Where do you want to go and what time?"

"I'll meet you in the lobby of your hotel about seven thirty. There's a great little place I know in the old town. I'm sure you'll love it."

Nick hung up and took a bottle of cold beer from the mini bar. He wrenched the top off with his thumb and forefinger and saluted himself in the mirror.

"Just like clockwork, partner. Everything is going just fine," he told his own image.

Chapter 8

The coffee, the first of many that day, soothed Etienne Delvaux somewhat, helped by the cigarette. He shuffled through the papers again. One had left a spark of interest in his mind. A message from Interpol headquarters in Lyon, sent as a courtesy and as a potential warning, advised of a series of jewellery shop hold-ups between Paris and Lille. Two of the robberies had resulted in violence. A man had been clubbed on the head with a gun in the Paris suburb of Bercy. Another shop keeper had been shot in the leg in the centre of Lille.

The perpetrators of the Bercy robbery, the message advised, were possibly a man and a woman in their early twenties. He was short, about 1.7 metres tall, with sallow skin, possibly French, probably Arab. His accomplice was thought to be either American or English. She spoke English well and French badly, with a strong accent. Her height was given as identical to the man's. No other descriptive details were available. An eye witness in Lille insisted a woman with long, blonde ringlets had run from the shop and jumped into a black BMW. The driver was said to be dark skinned. A note, added later, concluded that similar robberies had taken place in the USA over the past year.

The perpetrator in each case had been a woman with long, blonde hair, or long, black hair, or short, blonde hair or short, black hair. There was no mention of an accomplice, male or female, in the American robberies.

Etienne shook his head in amazement. Rarely had he seen such a vague and confusing description of suspected criminals. Either someone was totally incompetent, or those two, if it really was only two, were rather clever.

"Don't come here, whoever you are. Let the French look after you, please," Etienne prayed silently.

Already his mind was on the special diamond display scheduled for the Heritage Museum the following week. He didn't need any bent foreigners stirring up his patch. That damned *Namib Star*, unlucky for some, was already causing him enough worry. The Costa Rican insurance agent was driving him crazy with his interference. The owner had been barely coherent when they met to discuss security. From the look and smell of him he had been drinking steadily for hours. Delvaux had been tempted to lock him up just to dry him out. Instead he sent him back to the Hilton to sleep off his torpor.

A request for a security check on a visiting American photo-journalist was dealt with quickly. The request was passed to the Seattle police. Etienne had insisted that anyone who might possibly come in contact with the diamond be vetted by his office. It was only a formality, still, it kept him aware of potential trouble. The check came back later by fax with 'No Criminal Record' stamped on it. Etienne made a mental note to keep track of the American anyway.

At 09:30 Etienne stood in the centre of a bare room at the Heritage Diamond Museum. A black cross was marked on the floor at his feet. Coiled in the middle was a neat bundle of wires which disappeared into a plastic tube through the floor. Two doorways, without doors, afforded entry and exit to the room. A third door was marked as an emergency exit only. It was always electronically alarmed.

"The people will come through here, Mijnheer," curator Wim Cijfers explained, pointing to the entrance he and Etienne had taken. "They stand here, where we will have blue silk ropes as a retaining barrier, they look at the diamond on its pedestal here and leave through that exit." He pointed to the other opening.

"What else will be in the room? Any other display cabinets? Any other furniture?"

"No, only framed pictures of the Namib Desert, where the diamond came from, there'll be five or six of those on each wall, and then the *Namib Star* will be contained under its clear tempered glass dome."

Delvaux looked around him. He scanned the ceiling and the walls, determined to eliminate potential problems before they could occur. A thin shadow on the wall between the exit opening and the emergency door attracted him.

"What is this?" he asked the curator as he ran his thick black fingers down the vertical line. "It feels like a partition under this paper." He stepped back and studied the wall. The fine outline of a door was just visible.

"It is. It's an old doorway. It used to lead to the next building – the Diamond Institute," Cijfers explained. "Actually, it still does, only it's locked from the other side now and the corridor has been sealed at the other end as well, so it has no use as a door."

Delvaux rapped sharply on the door hearing a hollow muffled echo knocking back. He ran his fingers down the line again, noticing the paper had been cut to fit the door exactly.

"Show me the other end. I don't like surprises." Delvaux hitched up his pants as he spoke and motioned the curator to go ahead of him.

"All the buildings on this street are connected by doors, you know that, don't you?" Cijfers asked.

"Yes, I know. That's what worries me. Even with the surveillance systems, I still don't like it."

In the Diamond Institute, Delvaux examined the heavy steel door with the multiple combination locks at the other end of the corridor, satisfying himself that no unauthorized access was possible, short of dynamite.

"Let's take another look inside the museum. I want to check that emergency exit."

From the floor above the display room, Delvaux ordered the curator to open a window directly over the emergency exit.

"I can't, it's alarmed. All the exits are wired."

Swearing softly with frustration Delvaux looked through the window to the courtyard below and the surrounding walls.

"Is that gate alarmed?" He pointed to the end of the courtyard.

"Yes, it has a separate alarm so it doesn't trip those inside."

"What about the walls? Any pressure points, anything?" he asked hopefully.

"No, nothing, as far as I know. Only broken glass along the top."

"That's a great help. Criminals have been known to wear gloves."

"I'm the museum's curator, Inspector, not its security expert," Cijfers reminded Delvaux coldly. "I think you should talk to Ivo de Smet at Antigone Security, he's the expert."

"Yeah, sorry. I'll do that. Thanks for showing me around."

By the time the detective left Wim Cijfers was exhausted. "I'm too old for this," he muttered to himself as he poured a cup of strong black coffee.

Delvaux didn't leave immediately. He went back and took another look at that door to the closed corridor. Even though he could not see any way to open it from the side he was on, he didn't like the door at all. On the way out he spoke briefly with a shaven headed young man. He noticed he had a slight accent. Probably from England originally and educated here, he decided.

The security guard at the front door told him jokingly, "We've got plenty of footage of you now, Inspector. You block the whole frame."

Delvaux gave his customary grunt. He didn't have much of a sense of humour. "I'd like to see a copy of each video tape at the close of each day. Starting today and then every day until that

132

diamond leaves Antwerp. If your employer has any questions, he knows where to find me."

At the back of the building, beyond the wall surrounding the small courtyard, Delvaux stood with his hands on his hips studying the museum. The wall, he calculated, was a little over two and a half metres high. Standing on tiptoe he could touch the weather-worn broken glass embedded in the thin cement on top. It wasn't particularly sharp glass, certainly not enough to stop a determined thief.

Back in his office, Delvaux scribbled a note to recommend an extra security guard detail be posted in the courtyard, 24 hours a day, for the duration of the diamond's stay in Antwerp. He made a mental note to watch for the man with the accent and the shaven head.

* * *

The Paris police held a confusing file on two jewel thieves. They were believed to be a man and a woman working together. Fairly sure the woman was American, they asked for assistance from Interpol, the International Criminal Police Commission based in the French city of Lyon. They, in their turn, contacted the American state police forces. The New York State Police Department responded with a similarly confusing file. One thing was sure. A man and a woman had robbed jewellery stores in five American states in the past year. For the last month all had been quiet. Now, it appeared, France was suffering a similar spate of robberies. While the French police studied their situation, across the Atlantic, others were working on another side of the problem.

Midnight on a Sunday could hardly be considered part of normal working hours for most people. FBI agent Jack Philmore, however, saw nothing unusual in being in the office at that hour. All the lights were on in the Hoover Building at 935 Pennsylvania Avenue in Washington, DC. Other agents were equally hard at work on their own case files. Philmore closed his eyes and leaned back in his chair. There was a pattern. There had to be a pattern. All criminals, in his experience, worked to a pattern, even if they didn't recognize it themselves. He rubbed his eyes with the heels of his hands and yawned loudly.

In front of him, scattered across his desk were police and newspaper reports from five nearby states about robberies at jewellery stores. Jack Philmore routinely received copies of any and all diamond store hold ups in the States. His interest was partly professional, partly personal. The Cadillac Ben had stolen from the parking lot in Lebanon belonged to his father-in-law. A man had been murdered that day in a jewellery store. Agent Philmore had no doubt the two events were connected. His files, and the Pennsylvania police department files, suggested the unsolved crime had been perpetrated by two white Caucasian males, probably in their late teens.

"What is the connection, if any, between this robbery and all those in which a young man and a young woman were involved?" Philmore asked himself. Somewhere, he felt there was a link. "Could the eye-witnesses have been wrong?" he wondered aloud. "Could it be the same pair?"

Keeping that possibility in mind, Philmore began reviewing each file. He made a chart of the crime locations. Then he made another chart of cars reported stolen in those same areas on the day of the robbery or a day or two before.

The recent reports from France were disturbing. Three similar robberies had taken place in less than a week in Paris, one with violence. The following week jewellers in Amiens, Cambrai and Lille had come under attack. A man in Lille had been shot in the leg. There were no other reports of violence. However, in each robbery the woman, it was always a woman, had threatened staff with a pistol. Philmore began to see the pattern which had eluded police in five American states and two far different countries separated by a huge ocean. France, it seemed, had, for some unaccountable reason, inherited the American felons.

Philmore sent a message asking the Sûreté in Paris what they knew of the getaway vehicles used by the jewel thieves. As he suspected, the reply showed a different car used for each robbery. He went back to the first file on his list. A robbery in Niagara Falls, on the Canadian side of the border.

Rather than ask already answered questions about robberies, Philmore took a tangential approach. He requested a check on any accidents, or other incidents involving vehicles, particularly cars or trucks with US plates, on the day of the robbery. It was a long shot, but he felt it was worth the effort, if only for the process of elimination. The answer was not long in coming.

One, Ali Ben Rachid, an Algerian citizen studying at Cornell University, had been involved in an accident in Niagara Falls, Ontario, on the date in question. The information sheet stated that he had been alone at the time and was not at fault. The report advised that he had been driving a red Mustang and gave a New York State registration number. It also gave Ben's address and telephone number in Syracuse.

Philmore snapped his fingers in delight. "Gotcha baby," he shouted to the four walls of his cubicle. Immediately he sent off a request to New York State Police for a check on the car. Were there any outstanding tickets or traffic violations? Was there anything at all which might point yet another finger at the Algerian? A long-distance call to Ben's apartment revealed that he had moved without leaving a forwarding address. All bills had been paid, in cash, before departure. Somehow Philmore was not surprised. He was beginning to feel a grudging respect for this particular adversary.

Rapidly now the pieces of the jigsaw puzzle began to fall into place. He soon learned that Ben's Mustang had been found abandoned in a parking lot at New York's JFK Airport. Seven other vehicles had been dumped there the same day. Philmore asked for details of each car and its contents.

A Ford Bronco, parked not far from the Mustang, proved to have been stolen from the outskirts of Norwalk, Connecticut. Alarm bells began ringing in Philmore's head as he searched his files for another connection. A Ford Bronco had overstayed its welcome at a multi-story car park in Norwalk. It had been towed away to a police pound. On inspection a shotgun had been found under the front seat. A shotgun which, forensic experts would agree, had almost certainly been used in a fatal shooting at a jewellery store robbery in Harrisburg, Pennsylvania.

Philmore sent a message through Interpol to the Sûreté in Paris. In it he advised them there was a strong possibility that the spate of jewellery store hold ups in Paris and northern France had been committed by Ali Ben Rachid, an Algerian citizen. He included a full description and added a note that, although he believed the suspect had a female accomplice, possibly an American, there was no information available on her at that time.

Yusuf read of his friends' exploits in the daily newspaper and smiled. He had a job of a different sort for them. When Ben dropped in by himself late that night for a coffee, Yusuf was ready. Ben needed Yusuf. Without him he had nowhere safe to dispose of his takings. He didn't need or like Yusuf's attitude though. He went on the attack before Yusuf had said a word.

"Why the hell did you get April that gun? Don't you understand she's a menace with that thing in her hand?"

Yusuf laughed, "Don't worry, little brother. Everything is okay. She won't kill anyone. Now, I need you to help me with a favour."

"What?"

"I want you and April to leave a package on a Metro train for me. Someone else will pick it up."

"Why can't you do it? Why does April have to be there? Who will pick it up?"

"Listen to me, Ben. The less you know the better. Just do what I ask, for me and for Algeria. You owe me a favour anyway."

"What good will a package on a train do for Algeria?" Ben asked, his eyes suspicious as he chewed nervously on a finger nail. The answer dawned on him. "No one will pick it up will they? You don't want anyone to pick it up."

Yusuf didn't answer. He took a brown paper bag from under his desk and held it out to Ben.

"Take it," he ordered, "this is the package."

Ben shook his head, still attacking the finger nail. Yusuf placed the bag at Ben's feet and opened the top.

136

"See, just a cardboard box inside, nothing to worry about," he smiled icily at Ben. "Take it and do as I ask. But don't drop it."

"It's a bomb. Isn't it?"

"No more questions, Ben. Do as I say or, perhaps, the Sûreté will suddenly discover a few clues to the identities of the jewel thieves they search for."

Ben stared at Yusuf in dismay, assessing his opportunities.

"You want me to plant a bomb on the Metro, to kill people. Why are you doing this, Yusuf? I'm not a killer. I'm a thief, not a terrorist." Ben's thin voice rose as he wailed his increasing fear.

"This is for Algeria. For the past. There were so many wrongs. We must have revenge," Yusuf spoke softly, as if telling a child of the death of its mother, the words sighing with the weight of his feelings.

"Yusuf, that's all over. Long finished. Algeria has been independent for over thirty years. What can you possibly achieve by planting bombs now?"

"My father and my uncle, his brother, were murdered by the OAS, the Secret Army Organization, in 1962. They were working on the oil rigs at Hassi Touareg in the Sahara. They were blown to bits by an OAS bomb, Ben." Yusuf stood and grabbed hold of Ben's shirt with both hands. His eyes were wild and his teeth bared as he hissed his fury at history's interference in his youth.

"The French did nothing to help them or us, their families," Yusuf continued, tightening his grip on Ben's shirt front. "They even gave Raoul Salan, one of the OAS leaders, back his life, when they should have given him a firing squad."

Ben frowned, listening intently as the torrent of hatred burst from Yusuf's lips. Carefully, afraid to antagonize the man further, he pulled Yusuf's hands free and pushed him back a pace.

"A bomb on the Metro can only hurt innocent people, Yusuf. There must be a better way."

"Enough," Yusuf shouted. "You must do this for me, just this once."

He picked up the bag and placed it in Ben's hands.

"You will leave it under a seat on a north bound train leaving Châtelet station at eight o'clock tomorrow morning. You and April must leave the train at the next station and walk home. The timer is set to go off at 08:20. Now take it and go."

"I need another bag the same as this one," Ben said.

Yusuf looked at him strangely for a second, "Okay, Ben, I have another one."

He reached into a closet, took out a folded brown paper bag and gave it to him. Ben tucked the folded bag inside the bomb carrier and lifted the package gingerly. He left without another word. Though his fear of Yusuf was almost as intense as his horror of being blown to pieces, he certainly had no intention of keeping a live bomb with him all night. But he couldn't tell Yusuf that. Feeling sure Yusuf would be vindictive enough to expose him if he failed in his murderous assignment, Ben decided to place the bomb in the Metro as instructed. Only he would choose the station and the time. It was after midnight. With luck he could find a train on its final run back to the depot.

At Sentier Ben boarded an empty train marked Gallieni. He was sure the train would go out of service at that point and spend the night in a rail yard, or in the terminal station. Hopefully it would not be in use first thing in the morning. Making sure he couldn't be seen, he removed the folded bag and stuffed the bomb out of sight under his seat. Ben got off at the next station and watched as the four carriages rumbled out of sight through the black tunnel. With one hand in his pocket, the other holding an empty bag shaken out to look full, he walked back to the apartment with his head bowed. If any security cameras had picked up the image of a man entering a station or boarding the train with a brown paper bag he would also be seen leaving with it. April was fast asleep, curled in a tight ball in the middle of the bed, when Ben got home. He decided to sleep in the living room so as not to disturb her. He closed the bedroom door quietly and lowered himself wearily onto the couch. With the bomb on his mind, he knew there would be little or no rest for him.

Before daybreak, Ben and April were on their way out of the city. Ben signalled a right turn and sped down the ramp from the

Paris Periferique at Porte de la Chapelle. Keeping pace with the rest of the north bound traffic he settled back for a tedious drive. Beside him April was already asleep. The black Volkswagen Passat station wagon, he had discovered, was comfortable to handle over long distances; much better than the 2CV. Even more important, it too was an unremarkable car. There were thousands of them bustling along the highways of France, Belgium, Holland, and Germany. Ben had purchased the car second-hand from a Parisian dealer for just those reasons – plus the fact that April approved of it. No one was likely to take much notice of a Volkswagen.

On their last trip north they had selected targets at random. April enjoyed the haphazard method of closing her eyes and stabbing an index finger at a point on a map.

"There," she had announced, opening her eyes, "we'll go to Lilly."

"Lilly? It's not Lilly. L-I-L-L-E, it's pronounced more like Lill, or Leel," Ben corrected her.

"Whatever."

Ben shook his head in disgust at her lack of interest. "Come on, April, try saying it properly, it's important."

"Leeeeel," April drew out the name, prolonging the vowels to annoy him. Her mouth widened in an automatic parody of Ben's expression when he emphasized a word.

"That's not even funny. Keep practicing."

April had no intention of going to Lille again so she ignored the lesson and quickly forgot it. Her mind was fixed on new targets, wherever they might be.

For this latest journey, Ben intended being a little more scientific. No more picking points at random. He had done his homework thoroughly.

"I've been checking with the tourist offices," he explained to April. "There are vacation resorts all along the Channel coast. From France, into Belgium and all the way to Holland. That means money. There are casinos as well. More money. Wherever there's money, there will be jewellers. We're going to the sea."

Ben picked Le Touquet as his first port of call on the French side of the Channel. Boulogne, Calais and Dunkerque were next on his list. April decorated her map with gold stars above each of the cities on their planned itinerary. April slept most of the way to the coast, only waking up once to demand a stop as soon as possible. "I gotta pee real bad, and then I could use a cup of coffee and a donut, or something."

While April took advantage of a service station toilet on the outskirts of Arras, Ben turned up the car radio for a news bulletin.

"At ten o'clock this morning a bomb exploded in a carriage in the Paris Metro. As the train pulled out of Parmentier station an explosion ripped the carriage apart, derailing the two adjacent coaches. The carriage, in the middle of the train, only contained seven passengers at the time. One person is believed to have been killed and two others injured." There was no word on the possible culprits.

Ben sat at the wheel with his eyes closed. He had guessed at the package's contents. That's why he had disobeyed instructions and made the drop after rush hour, hoping to limit the damage. In some respects he had succeeded. He knew, however, that he had reached a turning point. There would be no going back to Paris for he and April now, Yusuf and his fellow terrorists would make life distinctly uncomfortable for them.

Ben and April moved along the coast following the tourist route. Without undue fuss, and without April getting violent, they raided jewellery stores in each city, In Oostende, on the Belgian coast, Ben learned of a fabulous blue diamond about to go on display in Antwerp. He showed April the newspaper clipping. "Look at this! Look at this!" he exclaimed in excitement. "This diamond is worth ten million pounds. That's over twenty million dollars."

April couldn't read the local newspaper, printed as it was in Flemish but, like Ben, she understood the money involved.

"Let's go get it, Sugar," she suggested.

Ben ignored her. He was deep in thought, weighing the pros and cons of an audacious robbery attempt. "Okay," he said.

140

"We'll go to Antwerp and see how it will be displayed. Antwerp is only an hour from here by car."

* * *

The old man shuffled along the street muttering to himself. Chris watched from the shadowy doorway of a building. As soon as the old man came in sight, Chris had checked his wristwatch. Exactly 08:30.

"On time as usual, Wim," he said under his breath. "I'll bet you've never been late for work, have you?"

Wearing scuffed black shoes, grey pants and a grey sweater, Chris was a nondescript individual topped by a mass of dark wavy hair. No one would remember much about him. He watched the old man approach, mentally recording every move, each subtle nuance of each footstep. His ears strained against the traffic noise for any sound made by his quarry.

The old man, dressed in a long black overcoat and a black homburg, stepped in a pile of fresh brown droppings.

"Fucking dog shit," he growled, stopping to scrape the sole of his shoe on the curb. Chris stifled a grin.

Turning towards a heavy glass door, the main entrance to a tall building, the old man wiped his shoe again on a large rush mat. A pigeon, roosting on the ledge above, chose that moment to relieve itself. A stream of greyish white liquid splattered on the homburg.

"Fucking pigeons," the old man grumbled, removing his hat and shaking it violently.

Across the street, Chris choked back his laughter. With a hand over his mouth, he sauntered away from the scene.

"I know I can do it," he told himself, still grinning at the old man's discomfort, "I know I can do it. He's a dream of a character."

Six days in a row Chris had spent watching and occasionally photographing Wim Cijfers, the sixty-seven-year-old curator of the Heritage Diamond Museum in Antwerp. On six successive days Chris looked like someone else. Each day he adopted a new hairstyle from someone he'd seen on the street. Each day he dressed to merge with the dull stone of the buildings. Yesterday he had been bald. In a fit of flamboyance, he'd shaved his head, not realizing just how damn cold it would be, even in late spring. Today the thick wig made up for his impulsiveness.

Chris walked briskly back to de Keyserlei and turned left, heading for the old town. As usual, Frankrijklei was a blur of speeding cars. Sensibly, he waited until the lights turned to green and made his way quickly across to the relative calm of the Meir pedestrian zone. Instinctively, without realizing he was doing it at first, he practiced the old man's shuffling walk. He talked to himself as he went, repeating the man's oaths at the mess on the pavements. Other pedestrians passed him with amused glances. He was oblivious to them all.

"Three more days, then I take over." Chris was nervous at the thought. He was also vaguely excited. The old man, Cijffers, lived alone in an apartment in the old city. He spent long hours at the museum and always dined alone at home. He almost never entertained and unexpected visitors were discouraged. Wim Cijffers enjoyed solitude. It gave him more time with his precious collection of rare books.

A quiet voice at his elbow forced Chris out of his reverie. "Meet us at the Pelgrim bar at eight tonight." Rupert didn't look at him: he spoke the words and kept on walking.

Chris went back to his hotel and had a continental breakfast of two croissants, strawberry jam, and a cup of bitter black coffee. Back in his room he changed into clean jeans, a white shirt and a grey Harris Tweed jacket. He discarded the old shoes in a corner and put on clean white running shoes. The wig, which he had taken off before entering the hotel, stayed in his backpack.

"Ready for phase two," Chris told his reflection in the bathroom mirror. Running a hand over his smooth head he decided he really wasn't ready to be permanently bald.

Chris paid the token admission fee and entered the museum. There was only one security guard on duty. He sat reading a magazine in front of a bank of five black and white television monitors. Chris smiled at his own image as he walked by. The security guard did not seem to notice him.

The first of four large interconnected rooms housed a series of pictorial descriptions of the diamond mining process. A cutaway model of black miners working in a tunnel at the bottom of a seemingly endless vertical shaft made Chris shudder. The very thought of spending eight or more hours each day in such conditions made his skin crawl.

"Not a job for the faint hearted, eh?" The deep loud gravelly voice smelled of stale cigarette smoke and yesterday's garlic. It spoke in Dutch. Chris, despite himself, jumped.

"Nee," he agreed.

Standing behind him, with weight lifter's shoulders topped by a thick neck and square face, was a huge black man wearing a grey suit. Chris took in the short, black curly hair, a little grey at the temples, the suit, white shirt and dark blue tie – and the serious expression.

"There's no way I could work down there, could you?"

The big man shook his head, patted Chris on the shoulder with a hand bigger than both Chris's combined and walked away without another word. Chris noticed the highly polished black shoes as their owner clumped through the door. Everything about the man shouted 'Cop!' Chris breathed a sigh of relief and continued his tour of the exhibits.

The entrance to one room was barred by a blue silk cord. Hanging from it, at knee height, was a sign announcing the room was closed. Chris leaned over the cord and looked into the forbidden space anyway. It was large, like a small ballroom, and it was empty except for a black cross on the floor and a bundle of wires. Now he knew where the diamond would soon be on display.

Chris sat in the second room while a television monitor on the wall told him all about the process of diamond extraction. He half listened to the Dutch explanation, his mind on more pressing matters. The door to the curator's office led from the same room. It was closed. Chris needed to have a look inside.

Boldness had to become his friend. He walked over and knocked.

"Kom," a muffled voice directed.

Chris opened the door into a small office, no more than three metres square. Book cases lined two walls, making the room appear smaller than it really was. An old desk against the far wall was piled high with papers. In the corner an antique wooden hat stand supported the black homburg and the heavy grey overcoat. Wim Cijfers sat at the desk with a ballpoint pen poised in his hand.

"Yes, can I help you?"

Artfully, making skilled use of his acting ability, Chris began asking questions about the museum. Claiming to be the newly appointed assistant curator at a similar establishment in a small Dutch town, he soon encouraged the old man to show his superior knowledge. Chris found his simple questions yielded long answers. He soon built up a detailed mental picture of the curator's daily movements. The old man, not normally given to needless conversation but sensing a fellow loner, had become garrulous.

When he left, Chris was armed with a mini encyclopedia of new facts. He knew where the diamond would be displayed. He knew it would sit on a pedestal mined with sensors. He knew the location of all the emergency exits. And, most important, he knew exactly the manner in which Wim Cijfers walked up and down stairs and through his domain. The only things he didn't yet know about his subject were highly important, but not impossible to learn.

"How," Chris wondered, "does Cijfers greet the security guard each morning and how does he bid him goodnight at the end of each day?"

He guessed that Cijfers probably did little more than grunt at them, if he acknowledged them at all. He would find out in the morning by being close when the curator arrived at work.

The cellar pub was crowded when Chris walked down the stone steps into its dark, red brick interior. Candles, set into cast iron frames on the walls, cast eccentric beams across long

144

wooden tables filled with wine and beer glasses. In a corner, a hand was raised as Chris stepped past a rack of spluttering flames. Stepping over the end of a bench, Chris manoeuvred his way to Rupert and Charles. He shook hands with them both and sat down facing his accomplices. They already had a glass of white wine each. Chris hailed a passing waiter. "Ein Bolleke, alstublieft," he ordered.

"Tomorrow night, at nine o'clock, we'll do the switch," Charles took the initiative. "We have a change of plans. There's a photographer who has permission to photograph the stone the night before the exhibition opens to the public on Monday. A few members of the press will be on hand. You need to be there. So will we."

Chris accepted his beer from the waiter and took a long draught of the bitter-sweet brown liquid. "How will you get in? Or do I simply open the door for you?"

"Don't worry about that now. The less you know the better. Just be ready in time tomorrow, we'll explain it all then."

Charles added a sensible suggestion, "You'd better check out of your hotel early. You can leave your bag in a locker at Centraal Station."

The three downed their drinks, paid the waiter and left. Chris wandered down the uneven cobblestones to t' Vagant, a pub where students often gathered until late at night. As usual it was busy. Chris ordered another Bolleke and sipped it thoughtfully, taking his time, content to listen to the babble of voices around him. On the way back to his hotel he stopped for a couple of slices of tangy pizza, begging the chef to put extra pepperoni on them. He ate both as he walked, still copying the curator's mannerisms.

There was little sleep for him that night. He closed his eyes and recalled the old man's walk, his funny shuffle, his voice, the way he wore his clothes. Chris knew he was ready. He'd never fluffed his lines on opening night; he wouldn't start now.

As he had suspected, Cijfers did not greet the security guards when he arrived at work in the morning. He waved a hand at them, nothing more. Getting through the rest of that day was a nightmare for Chris. With a bulky pack on his back he wandered to the station and checked his bags into a locker. For the next few hours he stayed in the old city, getting lost for a while in the narrow lanes of the all but deserted red light district. Late in the day he collected one of his bags and made his way back to the Diamond district. Not until he had discreetly escorted Cijfers home, from the other side of the street, did he really begin to relax.

At a few minutes before nine Rupert and Charles entered the narrow cobblestone street from the direction of the Cathedral of Our Lady. Charles kept watch at the corner, ready to warn of any approaching danger. Hidden in the shadows, with Rupert holding a mirror and a photograph, Chris quickly applied his makeup of latex wrinkles and bumps. Greasepaint, deftly applied, assisted the transition. A wispy grey wig completed the metamorphosis. In a matter of minutes he had become an old man. He pulled a black homburg and a long black coat out of his pack and dressed hurriedly.

"Okay," he asked Rupert, "how do I look?"

"Ugly, but you'll pass for now."

With adrenalin pumping and heart beating faster than normal, Chris mounted the stairs to the top apartment. Behind him, Rupert and Charles kept to the shadows. Chris rang the bell three times before a muffled voice urged him to be patient. Wim Cijfers unbolted his front door and came face to face with a mirror image of himself. The curator's mouth fell wide open.

Chris pushed him gently back into the room as a look of utter confusion creased Wim's already wrinkled features. He stared at his double, trying to understand. So astonished was he that he failed to notice Rupert and Charles until it was too late. Rupert crossed the three paces between them and clamped a chloroformed pad over Wim's nose and mouth. In seconds, the old curator sagged against him without making a sound.

BOOK 4

The Rendezvous

Chapter 9   Antwerp

The *Namib Star* sat on its illuminated pedestal at exactly the right angle. The artfully placed lighting eliminated all shadows, allowing the icy, imperial brilliance of the diamond to dominate the large room. On the walls a series of framed colour photographs of the Namib Desert transmitted a suggestion of latent heat to compliment the stone. One man stood alone in the room – on duty. The security guard checked his watch again: another hour before the photographer and his party would arrive. He was bored and getting tired. Late shifts always irritated him, he would much rather be at home, or in a bar drinking Hoegarden white beer with his friends. Already he had been on duty for three hours. He had studied the diamond from all angles, ever since the rich, fat owner had placed it on the silk cushion with sweaty hands. He had no further interest in the room, except to have the evening over.

"Hey, Herman, take over for a minute will you? I need to go for a piss," he called to another guard reading a newspaper near the entrance door.

Outside the dark grey sky settled heavily on the roof tops.

The evening was young, barely ready to give way to the night. The weather insisted on gloom. Rain, which had been falling for most of the day, continued without a break. Cobblestones glistened, reflecting the glow of neon lights from bars and restaurants. A tram swayed and rumbled down the middle of the street, adding its own lights and reflected image fleetingly to the neon signs. Cars splashed by, sending sheets of cold dirty rain water over the pavements. Pedestrians, huddled under a rainbow of umbrellas, swore bitterly as their shoes and ankles were flooded by callous drivers.

Inspector Delvaux arrived at the museum soon after the fake Wim Cijfers walked in with the two antique dealers posing as Sotheby's agents. Half an hour later Ben and April walked towards the same entrance arm in arm huddled under an umbrella, planning to look at the building and its security from the outside. The diamond would not be on public display until the following day. Ben planned to be among the visitors on opening day and, if he saw an opportunity, attempt the theft in mid-week. Ahead of them, Nick and Sam shook the rain off their shared umbrella and pressed the buzzer on the museum's door. Ben pulled April across the road and kept walking.

"Did you see that?" he whispered. "Those two were let in. There must be something going on in there tonight. Maybe it's a special showing. Maybe we can just walk in behind those two and take the diamond tonight. Let's try."

At the sound of the buzzer April pushed open the main door to the museum with Ben right behind her. Two security guards greeted them without expression. The one by the electronic arch received a dazzling smile from April, which he instinctively returned. April leaned over the counter, as if to say something to the seated guard. Three buttons of her blouse were open and her breasts were plainly visible as she bent forward. Her back blocked the other guard's view.

The guard by the arch motioned Ben to come forward and show his pass as April went into her act. Her short skirt rode up, showing shapely calf muscles, the backs of her thighs and a glimpse of white panties. Ben's pass received no more than a

148

cursory glance, the guard's eyes were far too busy. Behind the desk his partner opened his mouth to say something and the shiny silver barrel of a pistol was thrust in.

"Suck on this, Buster," April snarled softly, "and put your hands on the table or you're dead."

While one guard was distracted, ogling April's legs, Ben forced an identical pistol to his septum, bending the guard's nose up and back.

"Don't move, don't make a sound," Ben whispered harshly in French.

With his left hand he drew the guard's revolver and stuck it in his own belt. "Now, sit on the floor, quickly."

"Ready, Ben?" April called, her voice harsh with adrenaline, keeping her eyes on the lips sucking her pistol.

"Yeah."

"Okay, now!"

April almost ripped a tooth out of the guard's mouth as she removed the barrel in one lightning motion. She reversed it and clubbed him on the head as Ben dealt silently with the other.

April took her victim's gun, holding it in her left hand, her own pistol in her right. Ben signalled her to walk round the security arch behind him. They entered the display room with guns at the ready at the very moment Nick let off a flash. For a split second everyone was frozen, statue like, in a sculptor's tableau, caught on film by a fraction of time.

"Nobody make a move," Ben shouted, pointing his gun at a big black man who had one hand suspended between his waist and the inside of his coat. April, cool as could be, disarmed a third security guard before he remembered he had a gun.

"Okay now, everybody, face down on the floor. You," Ben shouted at Etienne, "get down, now, or I'll shoot."

Delvaux hesitated a moment longer, never taking his eyes off Ben. April shot him in the fleshy part of his right thigh.

"He said down, you bastard. Are you deaf?" she screamed.

As Delvaux hit the floor he rolled left on to his back, drawing his service revolver as he did so. Ben watched in horror as the muzzle came up and spat death in his direction. He saw the gun.

He saw the opening from which the bullet had to come. He heard the sharp retort and, he thought he saw the bullet in flight. He'd never been hit by a sledgehammer. With his last fleeting seconds of life he realized what it would feel like. The blow to his chest numbed his body from navel to brain. Ben was vaguely aware of his legs letting him go as his torso jerked violently back against the wall. Dimly he saw April staring at him in shock as he tried to stay alive. He heard more shots. An image of Warren Beatty and Fay Dunaway hanging in a grotesque tableau out of a bullet-ridden car in the movie *Bonnie and Clyde* passed his eyes. Everything went fuzzy, then grey, then dark, as his brain entered a long, narrow tunnel which had no end. Sliding down the white wall Ben left a thin smear of bright red Algerian blood as a testimony to his passing.

All the lights went out as Ben died. They flickered on again as a backup generator kicked into action, flashed a couple of times and went out as the generator died. Chris, praying the lack of power had disengaged the electronic alarm system, half stood and stretched out his hand for the diamond. He scooped the gem from the cushion as a body brushed against him. The diamond was torn from his grasp.

Delvaux risked a second shot at where April had been – the only one who, he guessed, was still standing. He missed. The bullet ricocheted off Nick's tripod with a high-pitched whine and buried itself in the wall above Ben's head. Sam grabbed for the camera as the tripod toppled over her legs. All she got was the flash unit. Her thumb pressed the test button without knowing it.

The sudden brief glare lit up the room, showing April crouching by Ben's body, Nick on his feet moving past the detective towards the entrance, a faint shadow on one wall, two figures under the emergency exit sign, Tango huddled against a wall near the disarmed security guard, and the curator at the pedestal. April fired three times without aiming, hearing someone swear, seeing the photographer spin against a wall holding his arm. Delvaux, still on his back, fired directly at her, hearing the smack of the impact followed by a deep sigh. Chris launched himself full length across the floor and skidded into the doubtful protection of the wall.

April sat down hard, her legs splayed out, her skirt up, all the breath knocked out of her. There was a fire burning in her abdomen and a thought probing at her mind. "Now Ben won't be able to buy me a puppy." Slowly she raised her right hand and tried to aim her pistol at the black man on the floor. He had killed Ben and he had tried to kill her. Now he must die. For some reason she couldn't hold the barrel still. She clasped her left hand round her right and tried again. The barrel continued to waver as April's eyes began to close. She shook her head once, trying to concentrate, trying to ignore the pain spreading through her body. Squeezing as hard as she could, her right index finger pulled the trigger as the gun's barrel drifted across the room in a small arc. The bullet ploughed a furrow in the hardwood floor before screaming over Delvaux's head and smacking into the far wall. Delvaux, still in the same position, gritted his teeth at his own pain and winced as April's bullet fanned his forehead. He took a breath, held it, and pulled his trigger again. April took the second bullet through the bridge of her nose and died thinking of the dog she'd never had.

"Get some lights on," roared Delvaux. "Get some damned lights on in here."

The security guard found the master switch and the room flooded with light, making all eyes blink at the sudden brightness. Cautiously Delvaux looked around him. April lay on her back in an ungainly posture, legs wide apart, her head bleeding on Ben's lap. Propped up by the wall, Ben's body had merely slumped, his head was bowed as if trying to kiss April.

Nick sat against a far wall cradling his right arm. Blood trickled down to his pants and ran to the floor in a small pool. Sam lay still on the floor near him clutching the camera, her eyes wide and scared. The curator crouched against a wall, his hands over his ears. Tango Perez lay in a heap, facing away from the scene. A hole in the back of his head dribbled his life blood and his brains onto the polished wooden floor. No one else was in the room. The emergency exit door was half open.

Delvaux dragged himself to his feet, reaching out to his security guard for assistance. He stared at the pedestal. The clear glass cover was off. No hint of blue fire remained. No dazzling sparkle. The pedestal was barren. Only a small velvet cushion and the cover, lying on the floor nearby, suggested the diamond had ever been in the room. In the foyer, unaware of the drama, two stunned guards sat on the floor trying to revive themselves.

"I'll phone for help from my office."

Delvaux dimly heard the voice, the movements attracted him more. As the old curator ran across the room, he jumped over Ben's outstretched legs and took the three steps to the adjoining room in one bound. Delvaux watched him curiously, his attention sharpened by the pain in his leg, as he leaned on the guard's shoulder.

"Go with him," he told the guard, indicating the curator. "Don't let him leave his office. Nobody else moves."

The security guard hesitated, looking first at Delvaux, then at the direction the curator had taken.

"But..." he started.

"Go on. I'll be alright," Delvaux straightened his back and pushed the guard. "Go," he said.

Limping, with blood trailing on the floor, Delvaux pushed open the emergency exit a little more with his shoulder and looked into the night.

"Armand," he called. A groan from the far corner of the courtyard greeted him.

"Armand, is that you?" he called again.

"Yes, Inspector, I'm here," the voice was slow but strong enough. "I'm coming."

Limping, Delvaux made his way to April and Ben. Expertly he checked for vital signs, finding none. He examined Perez perfunctorily, knowing he had died instantly.

"You okay?" he asked Nick.

"No, I've been shot in the arm."

"You'll live. I want all the films you shot tonight, now. Can you empty the camera, or shall I do it for you?"

"Hey, wait a minute," Nick howled, "that's my work for

chrissakes. When will I get them back?"

"When I say so. Don't worry: you'll get them back, eventually."

Sam rewound the film in the camera and took it out while Nick fished in his camera bag for other films. Delvaux held out his big hand and took the lot, slipping them into his jacket pocket.

"I'll give you a receipt later," he growled and turned away towards the curator's office, grimacing with pain as he took the steps one at a time. As the wail of approaching sirens filled the air, Delvaux lowered his bulk into a chair and faced the curator.

"So, Mijnheer," he began. "We need to talk, eh?"

Chris sat opposite at Wim's desk, his face ashen, his legs and hands trembling uncontrollably. He nodded, his eyes staring at the blood seeping from the detective's pants.

"Who are you, Mijnheer? Who are you?" Delvaux asked with a sigh, "I know you're not old Wim Cijfers. He couldn't move as fast as you if his arse was on fire. Who are you, Mijnheer?"

Slowly Chris pulled off his wig and let it fall to the floor. His stubble of new hair stood erect with the hot perspiration born of intense fear bubbling around it. With one hand, he peeled a thin layer of latex off his face and dropped it on the desk. He tore a small lump of the same material from the side of his nose and another from his chin.

"Ah, so," Delvaux scowled. "We have met before, have we not?"

Chris looked across the desk at Delvaux, resignation on his face.

"Yes, we have," he said quietly. "My name is Chris Montague, I'm an actor."

BOOK 5

The Reprise

Chapter 10

Antwerp. One year later.

"How the Hell did it all go so wrong? I did my part. I got them in. I made the grab for them. Christ, I worked so hard on this bloody job. For two seconds, two bloody seconds, I held it in the palm of my hand. What the Hell happened? I still don't understand it, Miss Walker, do you?"

"Please. Call me, Sam."

Chris ignored the interruption. He paced up and down the dull interior of the damp interview room, his long arms flailing the air as he talked, not really expecting an answer.

Sam waited for him to settle down again. Waited for his dark eyes to return to hers. Seven paces one way: a short walk for a tall man, then an about turn and another seven paces. He threw a glance at Sam, sitting at the table, listening. Chris ignored the tape recorder and its miniature microphone, even though his words, his anger, were being taken from him and held captive, even as he was a captive. Still he disregarded it, as he would an overhead microphone on a stage. Subconsciously he was acting, playing to his audience of one. Desperately striving to make her believe in him, and in his character.

Above his head a single light bulb, hanging from beneath an old fashioned conical shade, like a flattened Chinese hat or a dusty upturned saucer, cast a modest glow without offering any warmth. The greying paint, which had once been a clean and bright white, showed the room's age unkindly. The old wooden table and two chairs would have been rejected by most kitchens as unsanitary and unsafe. Carved and scarred with the names of decades of miscreants, real and suspected, the rickety furniture suited the room. Neither showed any character or style. It wasn't a pleasant space.

"If it hadn't been for me and my skills, my talents, they would have got nowhere. Useless berks. So much for a higher bloody education. Useless, the pair of them. And those other two, with the guns, where did they come from? Talk about your bloody dangerous amateurs."

Sam watched Chris as he ranted, only half listening to his angry soliloquy – they'd gone over it so many times already. Idly she wondered about others, men and women, who had passed this way. Some would have been en route to lengthy incarcerations, some only stopping briefly before walking to freedom. Only that morning, as she arrived at the fortress-like prison on Antwerp's Begijnstraat, two armed members of the Rijkswacht – Belgium's national police force – were escorting a frightened looking, handcuffed prisoner through the green entrance door. She knew, as surely as the English actor did, there was little chance of freedom for Chris in the foreseeable future. She shuddered at the thought. Chris sat down across the table from her, pulling her abruptly back to the present as his elbows thumped onto the once shiny wooden top.

"I'm a good actor. I proved that, didn't I? Only a really good actor could have done what I did here, right? I may not have made much of a mark on the stage so far, although I've played in half the towns and cities in Britain. I got to the West End once too. Only a small part, mind you. But I got there didn't I?"

"Did you ever try Broadway?"

"Broadway? No, no chance. I'd like to have gone, mind you, but it's a long way to America. Takes a lot of money, that does.

If this job had gone right there would have been plenty of that. Broadway, you ask. Huh! Hammersmith bloody Broadway is about my lot."

Outside in the corridor a guard stubbed out his cigarette, dropped his magazine on the floor and stood up. He stretched, revealing elliptical damp patches of sweat on the underarms of his grey uniform shirt. With a bored expression, he opened the small square hatch to the interview room and looked in. The prisoner, facing him, glanced up at the sound. The woman either didn't hear or wasn't interested in the slight noise. She kept her back to him. The guard watched and listened for a few moments, finding difficulty in understanding the rapid English firing between the two. He closed the hatch and went back to his magazine.

"Tell me about the diamond again, Chris. How did you get involved? What made you come to Antwerp? What really happened to the diamond that day?"

"Oh hell, I don't know," he mumbled, scratching the short stubble he wore on his head instead of hair. "It was so chaotic, with people screaming and dying. And yet, somehow, deep inside, I feel I should know. I don't understand it though. You were there. Do you understand what happened?"

Sam shook her head. Chris didn't notice. He looked into the distance, through her, his gaze piercing between her eyes without seeing the woman. Holding his hands together on the table, he began picking at the remains of a finger nail. Noticing his chewed fingernails for the first time, Sam grimaced in distaste, clenching her fists under the table as if to protect her own carefully manicured hands. Chris started to say something. Changing his mind, he raised his right hand and gnawed on a finger. He gave her, or perhaps it was a memory, a half smile. His mind was wandering again, back to that day. Back to a different time, a better place.

"I can still feel that beauty you know. The one I held in my hand. Worth ten million pounds it was; that's what they reckon. Bigger than a bloody egg it was. Can you imagine? Ten million quid for a piece of coal? That's what it was once. I know, I read about it. They come out of underground volcanoes. This one had been lying around in an African desert for millions of years, until some darkie found it. He gave it away for a couple of cows. Two bloody cows! Can you imagine it? That was only sixty odd years ago. Now it's worth ten million. And I held it in my hand. It was cold, you know. Not warm like you'd think. Cold, like a stone in winter. How can anything be worth ten million quid? But it was and I had it in the palm of my hand. A bloody great blue diamond. Ten million pounds. Think what I could have done with my share. They were gonna give me half a million. That's what they promised. There's actors in Hollywood don't get anywhere near that much. I would have been a star immediately."

"Chris, if I'm going to help you write your story, if I'm to really help, you must keep on track, otherwise we'll get nowhere. Let's go back again. How did it all start? How did you get involved?"

"What? Oh, how did it all start? Well, it's a year ago now, almost. Yeah, a year ago next week. I wish I could turn back the clock, I really do. If I could I'd just do the bloody job myself. I know I could have got away with it. Those bloody chinless wonders – look where they landed me. And where are they now? Back home in bloody England, I suppose, dreaming up more bloody stupid stunts. And those two with their noisy guns: how did they get into the museum? Christ, they frightened the life out of me. They were shooting people. They must have been out of their flaming minds. And what happened to the diamond? One second it was in my hand, the next it was gone."

"Chris," Sam's voice had sharpened, she sounded a little impatient, as if she had no time to spare.

He looked down at his hands where a thin seam of blood trickled down one finger from the torn quick. He sucked it, licking it clean, wiped it on his grey prison issue pants.

"What? Oh yeah, how did it all start? Well, I've been trying to piece it all together for months. From newspaper articles, reference books and the like. I've written most of it down already, you know, the way I reckon it happened. It's just notes really. You should let your imagination work for you a bit. That's what I've been doing. It helps me try to understand. You're a writer: using your imagination shouldn't be difficult for you. If you've got the time, like I have, I'll tell you a story and you can use whatever you want from it."

Chris held up a large bulky manila envelope. "It's all here, you know, everything I could think of."

He pulled a sheet of white paper out and showed it to her. One line was scrawled across it in thick black letters.

THE NAMIB STAR

He dropped the heavy envelope and the piece of paper on the table in front of Sam.

"You can read it if you like. Or I can just tell you the story as I understand it."

Sam reached for the package and pulled out a stack of hand-written papers.

"How much time have we left?" she asked, looking at her watch.

"Less than half an hour. Not long enough to read much of it," Chris replied. "I reckon it really started over sixty years ago in southern Africa, where the diamond was found."

* * *

Sam reached for her cup of tea and sipped it. It had gone cold. Holding the pages of Chris's manuscript on her knees, she kicked off her shoes and made herself comfortable on the couch. Closing her eyes, she could almost feel the dreadful heat of the African sun sapping her energy, wearing her down. Without being aware of it, she wiped her forehead, imagining Kessler struggling for life after being struck by the black mamba. Hours later and still on the couch in her hotel room, Sam shivered. Pulling her sweater tightly around herself with one hand, she placed the last page of Chris's manuscript face down on the pile beside her. She bit her lower lip, wondering: was the *Namib Star* really an unlucky stone? Had the diamond really been responsible for Kessler's death?

* * *

"Where did you get all this information from?" Sam asked Chris at their next meeting. "You've been in prison for nearly a year and yet you sound like an expert on the diamond industry."

"I am, in a way," Chris told her. "There's nothing much to do in here, apart from study. I work in the prison library – and a couple of the guards have helped by getting other books and articles on diamonds for me."

"Well, I'm certainly impressed. There's a lot of hard work gone in to this story."

"One of the guards here has a brother who is a security guard at one of the diamond bourses. He has been a mine of information. Plus, I had some extra help," Chris volunteered.

Sam stared at him. "Extra help? From whom?"

"A man called Piet de Kerpel. As you have read, he cut the original rough diamond. He's very old now but he writes quite clearly and seems to enjoy our correspondence".

"Now I'm really impressed. How did you manage to contact de Kerpel? How old is he anyway?"

"My friend looked him up in the telephone directory. There's a few de Kerpels but we found him eventually. I phoned, told him a little about myself and asked if I could write to him. He said I could as long as I wrote in Dutch as his English spelling was not so good. That was months ago. We still write regularly, though I've never met him of course".

"He must be well into his eighties by now."

"He is. He's eighty-six, nearly eighty-seven, but his handwriting is beautiful, even though he had to teach himself to write with his left hand."

"Why his left hand? What happened to his right?"

"He lost it during the war."

"Chris Montague, you're amazing. No wonder you know so much about diamonds."

Sam looked at her watch. "I must go. I'll read some of this again tonight? And I promise I'll be back tomorrow. I'm not leaving Antwerp until we resolve this problem. I want to find out who stole the diamond and where it is now. I'll come to see you every day."

"Take your time, Miss Walker. I'm not going anywhere for a while," Chris answered quietly. "The diamond may be free, but I'm still a prisoner."

* * *

"All this stuff about Perez is fascinating, Chris," Sam leaned across the table towards him on her second visit. "Is it all true? Or did you make some of it up for a better story?" Sam smiled as she asked the questions but there was doubt in her eyes.

"Oh, some of the conversations are guesswork and some of the action. But the facts are real enough. I've had all that confirmed."

"Confirmed? By whom?"

"I wrote to Perez's home in Costa Rica. One of the other inmates here who speaks Spanish helped me translate the letter. Perez's valet, Carlos Gutierrez, replied, in Spanish of course, and he told me everything."

"Why would he go to all that trouble? He doesn't know anything about you."

"He does," Chris explained. "I told him about my part in the robbery and my dream of finding the real thieves and recovering the diamond. After that he couldn't do enough for me. He has a strong motive to help. He was named in the Tango Perez will as sole beneficiary."

"What about Sandy Anders, where did you get her story from?"

"Oh, she was easy," Chris replied with a broad smile. "Finding out about Hollywood stars, big and small, is no problem at all. Don't forget I have showbusiness contacts. She was easy to research."

"So she sold the diamond to Perez?"

"That's right. She sold it for a mint. Over two million dollars. That set her up for life." Chris scratched his nose and bit his lip thoughtfully. "She became quite successful after she left Campbell. Did you know she won an Oscar for one of her films?"

Sam shook her head, "No, I thought you said she wasn't a good actress?"

"No, she wasn't. She was terrible. But after she sold the diamond to Perez she became a film producer. That's how she won the Academy award. Then she died of cancer when she was thirty-nine."

"The unlucky blue diamond again," Sam chimed in.

"Perhaps. But, don't forget, for nearly twenty years she was extremely rich and she was successful. That doesn't sound unlucky to me."

"She was still young when she died. And Perez lost all his money."

"Miss Walker, Perez didn't lose his money. He threw it away. That man spent his millions on a flamboyant lifestyle. Champagne, caviar and girls ruined him. No, I don't believe the *Namib Star* is unlucky. Misfortune can happen to anyone. Diamonds have nothing to do with it."

"Well you've been unlucky. If you hadn't got mixed up with the antique dealers you wouldn't be in prison today."

"Luck didn't have anything to do with that. I was coerced into taking part and I did so. The fact that I got caught is immaterial. I broke the law. Now, much as I hate it, I'm paying for it."

"Tell me more about Tango Perez," Sam leaned forward expectantly. "What else do you know about him?"

"Perez is just one part of this story. Although a major part. If he hadn't gone broke, I wouldn't be in this prison and he might still be alive."

"What happened to him during the forty odd years between buying the diamond and his death?"

"I think his troubles began when he suffered a bad fall during a polo match in Los Angeles. His right elbow was so badly broken he was unable to play again. That's when he started

162

drinking. I believe." Chris smiled suddenly at Sam. "He had a great life you know, stacks of money, any girl he wanted, homes in three countries, and good looks to go with it."

"But polo was his life, wasn't it?"

"Yeah, Tango Perez liked being a star on the polo fields. He couldn't adjust to being on the sidelines. To compensate for his changed circumstances, he threw wild parties. One week he chartered a plane and flew a hundred hangers-on from California to Rio for a drunken orgy which lasted a couple of weeks. His valet estimated he spent close to a quarter of a million dollars on that bash alone. It doesn't take long to go through a fortune that way."

"Surely he had advisors, accountants and bankers, didn't they help?"

"No, not really. Perez took over his father's wealth when he died. He also divorced himself from all his father's business associates. He thought there was enough money to last forever. Unfortunately, the money, and his looks were only temporary."

"So, selling the diamond was the only way he could survive financially?"

"Yes, even then, if he had earned the ten million pounds, at least half of that would have had to go to his creditors. He lost a fortune and his life. And I lost my freedom."

"Chris, if we could find out who stole the diamond, or even where it is now, perhaps we could get you out of here," Sam gestured vaguely at the walls as she spoke.

"The police have been working on this case for a year now, all they know is that I was involved." Chris bit his lower lip and looked away for a second. "They haven't the faintest idea who stole the diamond or where it is. The thief, or thieves, and the diamond simply vanished."

"I'm a writer, Chris: a magazine writer. I deal in facts. I'm good at research because of that, as you are," she touched the papers between them. "There has to be an answer. Big blue diamonds don't just disappear into thin air. I'm determined to find out what really happened that night."

Chris shrugged his shoulders. Suddenly he looked defeated. He chewed at his nails again, staring at the wall behind Sam.

"The only way to get the answers is to learn everything possible about everyone who was in that room with the diamond. I've already told you the diamond's early history. But I don't know anything about the people who tried to steal it, or who could have stolen it."

"I can find out, Chris. I can." Sam reached for his hand and squeezed it. "Let's make a list of everyone who was there, apart from us, and what we know about them."

"Well, there were seven people as far as I remember, plus you and me." Chris nodded to Sam, "Okay, let's give it a try."

Sam drew two vertical lines on a sheet of paper. At the top of the left column she wrote 'name.' On the second she printed 'occupation.' The third she headed 'guilty/not guilty.' She wrote rapidly, the names all familiar to her. When she finished she had completed the first two columns.

"Now, Chris, are they guilty or not?"

Chris turned the sheet towards him and scanned the list. Beside Inspector Delvaux - Belgian detective - he wrote 'No.' On the following lines, beside the names and occupations he added his opinions of each.

Tango Perez – No (deceased)
Nick Gradowski – Photographer – unlikely
Ali Ben Rachid – thief – No (deceased)
April Young – thief – No (deceased)
Rupert Allen – unlikely but possible
Charles Berglund – unlikely but possible
Security guards – unlikely

"It doesn't help much, does it?" He turned the list back to Sam, "There's not a lot to work on there."

"Somewhere, in the background of one or more of these people, there is a clue, there has to be," Sam argued, "and I intend to dig until I know each person intimately."

"Where will you start?"

"I think with Nick Gradowski. I liked him, but I can't see any way he could have been involved. I'll get him out of the way first.

After Nick – who knows? Maybe I'll take a good look at Ben and April, they inadvertently brought in the FBI. They were prepared to kill to get the diamond."

"But we know they didn't steal it. They couldn't have," Chris complained.

"I still think it's important. I'll look closely at them anyway."

"Okay. While you do that, I want to consider someone else."

"Who's that," asked Sam.

"Nick Gradowski's contact at the Diamond Institute. Her name is Ingrid Strauss. I keep wondering if she has a place in this puzzle."

* *. *

A week later, Sam met with Chris again at the prison. "I've been reading your manuscript again," she said, "just looking for clues. You have a really good story, Chris. It's really good. Absolutely fascinating story, but we still don't know what really happened, do we?"

Chris shook his head, but he had a half smile on his lips.

"What? What have you found?" Sam pointed an index finger at him and asked again. "What have you found?"

"Not much, unfortunately. However, for what it's worth, I have discovered that Ingrid Strauss, the lady with the German name who worked at the Diamond Institute until last year, was born in Windhoek, South West Africa – now known as Namibia – in 1965. That's not suspicious in itself, although it is something of a coincidence."

"But the diamond was also found in South West Africa, in 1936, and by a young German – Franz Kessler. You wrote that in your book. Could there be a connection?"

"I don't know. I don't think so, but I'm waiting for some more information about Miss Strauss and her background. What have you found?"

"Nothing much of interest, except that Namibia has cropped up in my research, too. Nick Gradowski has travelled extensively in Africa on photo assignments for international magazines. He won an award a few years ago for a spread he did of scenes from the Namib Desert."

"I don't think that's significant. According to evidence presented at my trial, Gradowski and Strauss met for the first time only a few days before the robbery."

Sam shook her head in agitation. "Okay, so who do you think stole the diamond, Chris?"

"I don't know, Miss Walker. I really don't know." Chris leaned back in his chair with his hands folded behind his head.

Sam sighed and took a last sip of water from her Evian bottle. She rubbed her eyes, feeling the tiredness of too many hours of non-stop questions and not enough answers. Chris put his hands back on the table. He locked his fingers together, squeezing until the knuckles turned white.

"Let's look somewhere else for a moment. We need to know more about those two antique dealers, Berglund and Allen, or whatever their names really are, they set me up. They didn't need me to replace the curator at all. I was just a decoy. They already had fake ID cards saying they were with Sotheby's of London. They only wanted me there to take the blame. It didn't do them much good though, did it?"

"Someone got that diamond out of the museum, Chris. Are you sure it wasn't them?"

"Yeah, I'm sure. As soon as the shooting started they bolted. It was one of them who clobbered the guard outside in the courtyard. We need to look at them again, though."

Sam stared at Chris across the table, her head slightly on one side. She chewed on her lower lip and tapped a finger on the table but said nothing, although her eyes remained fixed on Chris, as if trying to read his mind.

He looked at Sam questioningly, "What are you thinking? Oh, no, Miss Walker, not me. I didn't steal it. I promise you that."

"I didn't say anything," Sam answered. "I'm just running all the names through my mind and wondering."

After a few moments of silence, Chris said, "I don't think anyone in that room stole it. I'm convinced there was someone else after that diamond. Not the crazies with the guns. Someone else."

Sam leaned forward, wide awake and alert again. "What makes you say that? You said something similar at the trial, didn't you?"

"Yeah, and no one believed me," Chris's eyes glistened with unshed tears. Almost a year in the Belgian jail had toughened him, but not completely. He closed his eyes and fought to regain control of his emotions. Sam sat there, unmoving, quiet, still thinking. Chris rubbed the tears from his eyes and looked up at the wall briefly. He turned back to Sam.

"Listen. When the lights went out I knocked the cover off the pedestal and grabbed the diamond. It was an impulse, nothing more. I suddenly thought I might get away with it in the confusion. The alarm didn't go off, that's what I can't understand," he stopped, his mind reaching back, knowing there was something else there, something important, something missing. With his eyes closed, he replayed the scene in his mind and started a hesitant commentary on what he was seeing.

"Someone turned off the alarms. We know that. Someone turned off the alarms. The police insisted it was me, as the curator. I didn't. I didn't even know how to. Somebody else turned them off. It had to have been the same person who turned off the lights. I believe it had to be an inside job."

"What about your accomplices, Berglund and Allen? Couldn't they have done it?"

"No, I'm sure they didn't. They probably planned to switch the alarms off at some point, but I think they were beaten to it."

"Yes, Chris, but by whom?"

"I don't know. Whose shadow was it on the wall? You remember you told the police you saw a shadow on the wall when you set off the flashgun."

"But no one else saw it and I could have been mistaken, there was so much going on," Sam closed her eyes and tried to picture the scene. "Was there someone else there? Who else could possibly have been in that room?"

There was no answer. Chris had his eyes closed as well and his mind went back to the robbery, searching for clues as Sam was doing.

"I only held it for a second, the diamond I mean. Someone wrenched it out of my hand. Somebody with long nails," he opened his eyes and stared at Sam's hands. Instinctively she closed her fists to hide the long, silver-painted nails.

"It wasn't me," she cried defensively.

"I know, you were on the floor by the entrance doorway with Nick, I saw you both. You couldn't possibly have crossed the room so fast. The police searched you anyway. They searched all of us."

Tapping his finger tips on the table, Chris closed his eyes again and tried to see back into the darkness of that room, that terrifying night.

"There was somebody else there," Sam could hardly hear him, he spoke so softly. "You are right. There was somebody else there." Louder now, he was getting excited as his memory fed him pictures from forgotten files.

"That door, the one without handles, I saw it close. I know I did." Chris slammed his hand on the table. "It WAS an inside job."

Sam looked confused. "Which door?"

"There's an old door in the wall, a few paces to the right of the emergency exit. It's so well disguised it's hard to see, even in daylight. It can only be opened from the other side. From there a long corridor leads to the next building – that's the Diamond Institute – and another locked door."

"How could you see it, then? It was dark."

"I know. It was dark, very dark for most people. But I can see quite well in the dark. I used to practice at home. It helped me get to my marks on a blacked-out stage without bumping into anything." Chris looked at Sam in triumph.

"I saw the thief. I saw the damn thief and I wasn't even aware of it at the time. Never. Not until now."

"How...?" Sam's question died as Chris interrupted her.

"That almost hidden door was opened from the other side – from the Diamond Institute side. I saw it as it was closing. There was a slight change in the blackness, a sharp angle, only there for a second. It was after the diamond was taken from me. Right after. I saw a head, just for a fraction, no more than two thirds of the way up the door. A head, with long hair, I think. There was a change there, too. Hair shines in the dark. Not much, but enough," he looked at Sam, his eyes hopeful. "I'll bet the thief had light coloured hair: blonde hair. And long nails. I'll take a bet it was a woman. In fact, I know it was a woman."

He thought for a few moments then looked up at Sam again. "That leads us back to …," Chris paused, thinking. When he started talking again, he almost stuttered, "Umm, Mi – Miss Walker, I know we've talked about her, and she was not in that display room with us, however, did you ever meet Ingrid Strauss?"

Sam stared at Chris. "Ingrid Strauss? Yes, I met her briefly through Nick Gradowski. I had to get a press permit from her office. We've already established that she was born in Namibia but…Are you suggesting she was involved?"

"Yes, Miss Walker. That's exactly who I think was involved. She has long blonde hair and beautiful long nails. I noticed them at the trial. And now I'm beginning to wonder about Gradowski."

"No," Sam shook her head. "I can't believe Nick was involved. He's a magazine photographer. Remember, he didn't even know Ingrid until he arrived in Antwerp. You said so yourself only a short while ago."

"Yes, I did. But are you sure?" Chris asked. He leaned forward across the desk. "Are you so sure that Nick and Ingrid didn't know each other? Because, suddenly, I am not. I think I saw them sharing a bottle of wine in a small bar in the back streets near St. Borromeo's Church while I was walking the city studying peoples' mannerisms. I remember the couple I saw seemed kind of cozy."

Sam shook her head. "I don't believe it. I don't believe it," she said quietly.

"I do," said Chris. "If those two could be tied together in some small way, the diamond's disappearance begins to be understandable."

Sam shook her head. "I can't believe it. I really can't believe it."

"Look, we need to know whether Nick and Ingrid were ever in Namibia at the same time. What year did he win that award, can you find out for me?"

Sam nodded. "Yes, that's easy. We also need to know when Ingrid left Namibia and when she arrived in Antwerp."

"And we need to know when she started her job as administrative director at the Diamond Institute," Chris added. "Can you get that information as well?"

"Yes, I think I can."

Sam and Chris stood up together and hugged each other spontaneously across the table.

* * *

Back in her hotel room, Sam called the Optimum Stock Photo Agency in London and asked for the dates on the images from Nick Gradowski's prize-winning photo essay on Namibia. The answer came back in seconds. She thanked her informant and hung up the phone.

"Now," she said aloud, "Let's go and find out more about Miss Ingrid Strauss."

Getting that information was considerably more difficult. Ingrid had left the Diamond Institute a few weeks after the robbery that had taken place in the adjoining building. No one knew where she had gone. Sam's attempts to find out how long Ingrid had worked there, and where she had come from failed. She tried a different approach. At the end of the day, she followed two young men from the institute to a nearby bar and sat across from them as they drank beer and talked. After a few minutes, one of them looked straight at her and smiled. Sam smiled back.

170

And that's really all it took, Sam reflected afterwards. Two smiles and an invitation for a drink. Getting information out of the two young men was easy. Sam learned that Ingrid was believed to have left Namibia in late 1985 and joined the Diamond Institute staff in the spring of 1986. Back in her hotel room, Sam wrote Ingrid and Nick's names on a sheet of paper. Ingrid was in Namibia when Nick received his award in Windhoek.

Through the stock photo agency contact in London, she requested a news photo of Nick with his prize in 1985. It arrived by courier two days later. Four people were in the photograph, Nick and the tourism minister for Namibia stood together in the middle. To Nick's left was another Namibian dignitary. To the tourism minster's right stood Ingrid Strauss – an employee of the tourist board.

Sam sat still, staring at the photograph for a long time, willing the evidence to tell a different story. Accepting there was no doubt, she made another call. One day later she had Ingrid's family tree from Namibia. Among the various members of the Strauss family was a reference to Kessler. Ingrid's mother was Franz Kessler's great niece. Was that coincidence? Sam wondered. Was it coincidence that Ingrid and Nick had met in Namibia in 1985? No, she decided. Ingrid and Nick had gone to extreme lengths to deny any previous relationship with each other.

Hurrying along the grey, wet cobblestone streets of Antwerp, Sam looked up at the sky, willing the clouds to part and let the sun shine through. It was still raining lightly when she entered the prison.

As soon as Chris was brought into the interview room by a guard, Sam turned on her recorder and began to detail her story. Chris listened in silence, his eyes never leaving Sam's face. When she finished her report, he got up and walked to the wall and back. He stood there, wordless but with a smile on his face; then he said, "Just as I suspected. Ingrid Strauss and Nick Gradowski. Now, how do we prove it?"

"We can't prove it, but we can give all this latest information to the police so they can do it," Sam suggested. "We have to tell Inspector Delvaux, Chris. Maybe they'll re-open the case. You'll be free."

"No, I won't," Chris sat down again, his excitement gone, "I won't be free. Don't forget I still helped kidnap old Wim Cijfers. They won't let me go. But, if I'm lucky, they just might reduce my sentence a bit."

"Yes, you're right. Let me tell Delvaux, please? All the evidence is here, in the photograph; in my files and here," she indicated the recorder.

"Okay, Miss Walker, we'll do it your way. Did you get all that on tape?"

"Yes, I did. I got it all. Every word."

"Then go tell Delvaux. Go tell him now. It's worth a shot."

For the first time in days, the sun was shining on the wet cobblestones as Sam left the prison for the short walk to the police headquarters.

EPILOGUE

The Denouement

Chapter 11   **The Namib Desert, 1996**

The early evening sun trailed the slim line of clouds over the horizon. Already streaks of yellow and gold, and flames of deep red, had begun painting the easy swell of the southern Atlantic Ocean far beyond the subtle pinks and grey shadows of the coastal range of dunes. In another thirty minutes darkness would fall and the over-heated desert would start to cool down.

Sixty years had passed since Franz Kessler had died on this high point of land. South West Africa, now known as Namibia, an independent nation, had seen many political changes in those decades. But its desert landscape had changed little. Each day the sun heated the dunes, sand, and rocks to scalding temperatures as it had done since time began. Each night, after the sun had descended into the cooling Atlantic Ocean, the darkness brought its own cold to add contrast to the barren land.

The creatures of the Namib Desert lived out their lives as they had always done and as they would always do, just as nature dictated. The noble oryx, singly and in groups, followed unmarked trails in their quest for food. The scavengers: jackals, hyenas and vultures watched for death and benefited from it, the way they had been born to do. Snakes and lizards warmed their cold blood in the sun while watching for prey to come close. The recumbent welwitschia plant ignored the seasons and the decades. Sixty years was a mere moment when added to the 2,000 years it had already lived, never moving from its birthplace on the flatlands between the dunes.

Where once Franz Kessler had planned to build his large, airy farm house there stood a modern, single-story ranch-style bungalow stretched out across the knoll. Surrounded by a high, white picket fence, there was no number on the gate; only a sun-bleached nameplate with the name STRAUSS in bold letters.

A year and three months had passed since the violence at the museum in Belgium. Nick sat on the bungalow's veranda, his camera and tripod close by. He put his bare feet up on the wooden rail and leaned back with his arms behind his head. His right hand rubbed his left arm thoughtfully, feeling the round scar of the healed bullet wound. His long hair hung loose around his shoulders. He was smiling, the setting sun making his face look darker than it really was. In the distance he heard the faint chop-chop-chop of a helicopter and wondered where it might be heading. There were no settlements or other homesteads within fifty kilometres of the house on the land that Franz Kessler had once owned.

In the half light of the room behind him a figure moved with hardly a sound. Nick heard the light pop of a Champagne cork, followed by the trickling of millions of bubbles. He turned and held out his hand. A tall, frosted glass with bubbles streaming over the side, greeted it. A slim hand with elegant fingers decorated with long, manicured nails pulled his hair back. Long blonde hair fell over his. Soft warm lips nuzzled his neck. Nick got to his feet and clinked his glass against another.

"Cheers, darling," he said. "Welcome home. It's been a long wait. Now we can start living."

The helicopter's rhythmic sounds intruded again, getting louder. Nick listened. Stepping sideways, he moved to the veranda rail and looked to the south and west. Red and green navigation lights showed for a moment as the engine noise faded again. He kept his gaze on the desert and the distant dunes for a few seconds more. The mechanical sounds wound down to nothing. The lights went out. Nick watched for many minutes, a frown creasing his forehead, but could not discern where the helicopter had landed, if in fact it had landed. The dunes could have muffled the sound of the engine, he reasoned, feeling a brief moment of concern. Shrugging his shoulders, he turned and raised his glass.

"Cheers," he repeated.

Ingrid kissed his neck once more. As Nick pulled her close, feeling her supple body molding itself against his, he looked over her shoulder. He took in the outline of the dunes, the shallow valley in between and the darkening sky. A slight movement to his left caused him to change his stance and the direction of his vision. There was motion out there in the dusky stillness.

Walking along the sandy track towards the house, only minutes away from the gate, their dark shadows elongated by the setting sun, were two men. One wore white tropical pants and an open-necked white shirt. The other looked out of place wearing a charcoal grey suit, white shirt and a dark tie. Even from where he stood on the veranda; even in the fading light, Nick could see the shine on the big man's black shoes. He straightened, holding Ingrid to one side.

"What is it?" she asked, following his gaze.

"Ah, shit!" Nick swore in a loud whisper. "It's that goddam Belgian cop, Delvaux."

The end

More fiction from Anthony Dalton

ALBERT ROSS IS LONELY
Praise for *Albert Ross is Lonely*

Albert Ross Is Lonely is an eloquent, evocative tale, simultaneously grounded in a tender and realistic love story and soaring with fine flights of allegory. Among the gannets, the gulls, and the guillemot colony up on the cliff resides the lone black-browed albatross (appropriately named Albert Ross) in the northern hemisphere. The journeys of Albert Ross are chronicled and photographed by Tripp, who came to the Scottish highland coast to study the majestic bird and to live out the last of days (his heart condition rendering his 48-year-old body in a weakened state). There Tripp encounters the lively and curious ornithologist Amanda. The exchanges between the cranky yet clever Tripp and quick-witted, disarming Amanda serve as one of the novels many pleasures. Dalton has a fine ear for dialogue and the delicate building of affection between the two is subtly developed.

Albert, Tripp, and Amanda are wonderful company for the reader. The rhythms of their individual and shared journeys ride the thermals as far as nature's forces allow.

I highly recommend *Albert Ross Is Lonely*. The last scenes manage to be concurrently inevitable and surprising – true to nature and true to these two individuals who for a time inhabit the rugged Scottish coast. Dalton is a smart and sensitive writer who has given the reader deeply invested characters and has written with the same integrity and commitment as those explorers who inhabit his fictional world.

Michael Hartnett
Author of *Fools in the Magic Kingdom*

THE MATHEMATICIAN'S JOURNEY

Praise for this work of historical fiction

Anthony Dalton is himself no stranger to the Arctic or sailing. He brings that knowledge to bear in his meticulously researched historical novel to take the reader on a voyage of discovery from the peaceful cloisters of Oxford of King James I's England to the Atlantic wastes and the frigid waters of what will come to be known as Hudson's Bay thence to a native village and finally , after many years, back to upper class London. Peopled with three-dimensional characters set against vividly described backgrounds the plot will keep you turning the pages and at book's end hoping the hero's adventures will continue in another work.

Patrick Taylor
New York Times best-selling author of
the *Irish Country Doctor* series

More fiction from Anthony Dalton

THE SIXTH MAN,
a raunchy tale of the old west

Narrated by outlaw Flo Quick, this book relates the adventures and misadventures of the infamous Dalton Gang of train and bank robbers in the 1890s of Kansas and what would become Oklahoma.

RELENTLESS PURSUIT

A zoologist hangs his career on a quest to find, capture, and protect a rogue tiger in the jungles of Bangladesh. Hampered in his quest by a rival, and distracted by a beautiful woman, the zoologist is in a race against time and the inevitable laws of the jungle.

Non-fiction books from Anthony Dalton

How to Become a Guest Speaker on Cruise Ships
Portraits of Bangladesh
Henry Hudson
Sir John Franklin
Fire Canoes
The Fur-Trade Fleet
Polar Bears
Adventures with Camera and Pen
A Long, Dangerous Coastline
Graveyard of the Pacific
Arctic Naturalist, the life of J. Dewey Soper
River Rough, River Smooth
Alone Against the Arctic
BAYCHIMO Arctic Ghost Ship
J/Boats Sailing to Success
Wayward Sailor, in search of the real Tristan Jones

184

ABOUT THE AUTHOR

Anthony Dalton is a Fellow of the Royal Geographical Society and a Fellow of the Royal Canadian Geographical Society. He is the award-winning author of 16 non-fiction books – most about the sea or about exploration – a series of short stories, and four earlier novels. A past President of the Canadian Authors Association, and an accomplished public speaker, he is an historian and former expedition leader. He lives with his family in the Southern Gulf Islands of British Columbia.

Manufactured by Amazon.ca
Bolton, ON

25853091R00109